Dear Inge...

*My father is about to be promoted to the rank of Obersturmführer.
And he says that the daughter of an SA Obersturmführer should
not be corresponding with a Jewess.*

He made me swear I wouldn't anymore.

*He said that when the Anschluss comes, many Austrians living
here will move back to Austria, and we will be among them. At
least he, Mutterl, and Heinz will. If I break my word to him, he
will leave me behind with his sister, Aunt Louisa. He has already
asked her if she would take me, and she said yes. . . .*

What good does it do to send B.S.L. and sign this,

Your Lieselotte?

"Orgel plays out her story with a musician's touch, the left hand
insisting on brutality and terror while the right hand maintains
the light step, the precise perceptions of a young girl; both hands
search each other out on the keyboard—crossing, parting, meeting, and parting again. Inge is a character who stays with you."

—*The New York Times Book Review*

OTHER WORLD WAR II BOOKS

The Devil in Vienna

DORIS ORGEL

speak

An Imprint of Penguin Group (USA) Inc.

Speak
Published by Penguin Group
Penguin Group (USA) Inc.,
345 Hudson Street, New York, New York 10014, U.S.A.
Penguin Books Ltd, 80 Strand, London WC2R ORL, England
Penguin Books Australia Ltd, 250 Camberwell Road,
Camberwell, Victoria 3124, Australia
Penguin Books Canada Ltd, 10 Alcorn Avenue, Toronto, Ontario, Canada M4V 3B2
Penguin Group (NZ), cnr Airborne and Rosedale Roads, Albany, Auckland 1310, New Zealand

First published in the United States of America by Dial Books for Young Readers, 1978
First paperback edition published by Puffin Books,
a division of Penguin Books USA Inc., 1988
Published by Speak,
an imprint of Penguin Group (USA) Inc., 2004

1 3 5 7 9 10 8 6 4 2

THE LIBRARY OF CONGRESS HAS CATALOGED THE PUFFIN BOOKS EDITION AS FOLLOWS:
Orgel, Doris.
The devil in Vienna.
Summary: A Jewish girl and the daughter of a Nazi have been best friends
since they started school, but in 1938 the thirteen-year-olds find
their close relationship difficult to maintain.
p. cm.
[1. Jews—Austria—Fiction. 2. Friendship—Fiction.
3. Austria—History—1938–1945—Fiction.] I. Title.
[PZ7.O632De 1988] [Fic] 87-7165 ISBN 0-14-032500-X
Speak ISBN 0-14-240236-2

Printed in the United States of America

The
Devil in Vienna

Author's Note

The political events in the background of this novel are factual.

The characters are fictional; that is to say, made up, as fictional characters usually are, of memories, imaginings, and aspects of actual people. For instance: Inge Dornenwald resembles my sister in some ways; in other ways, me, at thirteen. Her parents are based on ours. O.O. is the grandfather I wish I had had. Upstairs-Evi, by another name, lived upstairs from us, and actually was sent, alone, to Manchuria. There were several Mitzis. There was a Rabbi Taglicht; also a Father Ludwig, who took chances and saved lives.

I feel grateful to my parents, Ernst and Erna Adelberg, for lending me their memories; to my sister, Charlotte Lichtblau, for her participation; to Shelley Orgel, Marilyn E. Marlow, John Lichtblau, Dr. and Mrs. Leonard L. Shengold, and Father Richard Mann; to the Austrian Institute; and to Phyllis J. Fogelman, who wanted me to write this.

One

"But, Inge, they're predicting ideal snow conditions," said my mother. "Tommi Löwberg will be there. And besides, it's your birthday weekend. Be a sport, change your mind and come with us."

"You're probably the only girl in Vienna who'd turn down three days of skiing in the Zillertal," said my father, "but if that's what you want . . ."

Yes, I know it's peculiar, but that's what I want!

As for Tommi Löwberg, he and I can't stand each other. He's my parents' best friends' son—fifteen, handsome, and conceited, a fantastic skier; whereas I'd be mainly on my behind in the snow with my skis pointing at the sky, and he'd act very condescending.

Also, there's the composition Fräulein Pappenheim assigned us for Monday.

When I mentioned it, Mutti laughed. "Don't tell me that's why you're staying home. I've seen you write school compositions in less than an hour. You could write it on the train!"

Yes, but the subject of this one is very important to me. And Fräulein Pappenheim always tells us, "Reveal your real and true feelings." Well, for once I expect to, however long it takes.

Now comes my biggest reason: A feeling I have, impossible to explain, that I need to be here in Vienna on Sunday, because on

Sunday, my birthday, something might happen—I can't say what. I get goose bumps just thinking about it. . . .

My parents feel bad about my spending my birthday without them. So they're planning to be home in time for a late dinner on Sunday to give me my presents, which is very nice of them. And I couldn't even wish them Neck and Leg Break!

They stood in the doorway with their skis and poles and rucksacks on their backs, waiting. All it means is "good luck." I've said it lots of times before. But tonight, for some reason, I couldn't get the words out.

So I said, "I wish you the best powder snow!"

"Thanks" and "Be good" they said. Mutti reminded me that Opa Oskar (her father—I call him O.O.) is taking me out to a restaurant for supper Saturday night.

"See you Sunday evening," said Vati. "We'll be home by eight thirty if the train's on time. Don't get too impatient for your presents."

They kissed me; I, them. And they left.

On Sunday, the thirteenth of February, I'll be thirteen years old. So will Lieselotte. Two best friends turning thirteen on the thirteenth of the month—that's pretty rare, that has to mean something! And the day being Sunday, well, that just must mean something good! Oh, I know it sounds ridiculous, especially considering I'm really not superstitious. . . .

I remember exactly the look on Lieselotte's face when we discovered we had the same birthday. Her green eyes went wide and seemed to grow lighter, the color of unripe hazelnut shells.

Her light-brown eyebrows went up in amazement. I must have looked just as amazed. We were in the first class, standing outside the school by the iron fence, waiting, she for her mother, I for Kaethe, the maid we had then. "Can you come to my birthday party? It's tomorrow," we'd both said, then gaped, then laughed, then shouted it out loud to all the other little girls standing there waiting. Then Lieselotte ran up to her mother, shouting, "Mutterl, Mutterl," and told her. And I ran to Kaethe, shouting, "Kaethe, guess what! Lieselotte Vessely and I were born the same day!" We thought it was the luckiest thing, nearly a miracle.

We turned seven that year. I remember we thought of thirteen-year-old girls as grown-ups almost. Thirteen seemed centuries away. Little did I dream I'd still be so skinny that Mitzi sneaks lumps of butter into my soup when she thinks I'm not looking. Or that instead of a bosom, which most of my classmates already have, I'd have only two bumps the size of strawberries. Or that I'd still have a *Bubikopf* haircut—short at the sides, shaved up the back, ugly as an ogre. All the daughters of people my parents know wear their hair like that.

Lieselotte's hair was so long, she could almost sit on it. By now she probably can. . . .

After my parents left, I had supper in the kitchen with Mitzi and Fredl. Fredl is a fireman. Of all the admirers any of our maids have had, he's by far the nicest. I hope she marries him.

We had *Würstel* with mustard, hot sauerkraut with caraway seeds, leftover dumplings fried with egg, and beer. Fredl filled my glass to the brim.

"Not so much," said Mitzi.

"It won't hurt her, it's mostly foam," said Fredl.

Afterward I helped with the dishes. Then they asked me to play rummy with them, but they really wanted to be alone.

So did I, to start writing, and I wrote all this. Now I'm sleepy. It must be the beer. I think I'll sleep on my "real and true feelings." That way they'll be all ready to be revealed first thing in the morning.

Friday, February 11

It's a quarter past five. The sky is still black. I'm never up this early. (I'm not really "up" now either. It's still cold in my room; Mitzi hasn't put coal in the stove yet. So I'm sitting in bed with my blue eiderdown around me and this book propped on my knees.)

My room faces the courtyard. By day you can hear people beating carpets out there; children yelling; dogs barking; Herr Listopat, the janitor, calling his cat, "Striped Peterl, Striped Peterl!" And sometimes street musicians play accordions and sing.

Now it's absolutely still.

The stillness feels made especially for me, for writing "My Best Friend" in perfect privacy.

(Dear Fräulein Pappenheim,
Thank you for that subject!
Yes, I will reveal my real and true feelings, only I

can't get them down "in logical, orderly sequence," the way you want them. I have to let them come out any way they will. Also, I can't squeeze them into "three to five pages" of my composition notebook.

Therefore, dear old strict, fair Fräulein Pappenheim, I've decided to reveal them here, in this book of blank pages O.O. gave me for Christmas, I mean Chanukah.

But don't worry, I'll also write a composition, one you can accept. You'll give it a 2, maybe even a 1. And you will never know that it and what I write in here will be as unalike as an earthworm and a nightingale.

Your respectful pupil,
Inge Dornenwald)

Lieselotte Vessely and I met when we started school, and soon became the kind of friends who almost always know what the other is thinking, who trust each other and would rather spend time with each other than with anybody else.

But three months ago Lieselotte moved away to Munich. Three months is a very long time. And in all that time she has only written to me once. (I did also get a picture postcard of a dachshund puppy, postmarked *Regensburg, Germany,* and since I don't know anyone else in Germany, I assume she sent it. But it had no message, not even her signature, and the address was in block letters. So it doesn't count as writing to me, only as a mystery.)

I answered her letter immediately. I don't know whether she got my letter, or why she didn't write me again, or whether she has changed, or how. It's possible, it's even probable, she isn't my friend anymore. I'm more scared of that than of the Devil—in whom, of course, I don't believe anymore.

I don't know what made me bring *him* into this. . . .

No, that's not true, I do know: "Scared" always makes me think of the viaduct, and the viaduct always makes me think of the Devil—I'll get to that in a minute. Also, I've moved to my desk (my room is warm now, Mitzi lit the stove), still the same old knee-hole desk, painted white (I'm really getting too big for it), at which I wrote, or rather, began, my first story, which, it so happens, was about the Devil.

I was six and a half. We had just learned the alphabet in school, so finally, after only being able to make up stories in my head, I could write, or at least print. We hadn't learned script yet. It started something like this:

> WEN, THE, DEVILL, IS, NOT, HOME, IN, HELL, HE,
> COMS, TO, VIENNA, TO, VIZZIT, AND, DO, THINGGS,
> HERE. I HAVE, ALLREADY, SEEN, MANNY, PLAICES,
> WHERE, HE, WAS. FOR, INSTANZ, IT, IS, HIS, FAULT,
> THAT, THE, SECOND, TOWER, OF, ST. STEPHEN'S, IS,
> ONLY, SO, SHORT.

I was so wrapped up in printing all those letters, putting all those commas in, I didn't hear the door or the footsteps. Suddenly I smelled the Mutti smell: Eau de Cologne mixed with Memphis cigarette smoke. She stood reading over my shoulder. "That's very good, Ingelein," she said. But the look on her face said it was very funny.

People who can write are lucky, Mutti told me. They can put their fears and worries and secret bad feelings into stories and get over them that way.

Not if other people tiptoe up behind them and sneak looks, I thought.

She said, "Who knows, maybe you'll be a writer when you grow up."

I felt crushed. I'd thought I already was a writer! I crumpled up the Devil story and threw it away.

About the viaduct: It's a railroad underpass two blocks down from where we live, connecting our street to the street behind the tracks. I was never, never to set foot in it alone. So, of course, I wanted to.

Across from the viaduct, on our side, is Wegner's Grocery Store.

One day in October, the year I was in the first class, I went to Wegner's with Kaethe. She went there every chance she got. She spent hours in there. I waited outside.

I waited and waited, gazing over to the entrance of the dark, forbidden place. Finally I couldn't stand it anymore. I crossed the street—something else I was not supposed to do on my own. And I set foot inside.

It looked black as a coal mine. I thought, If a train passes overhead, it will sound as loud as the whole earth shattering apart, even if I hold my ears. Actually, I held my nose. It stank as if all the dogs from the whole Third District came in there to pee. But that was just ordinary-awful, as I'd expected. That was nothing yet.

Suddenly there came a noise, *Krrrtttzzz!* (A match being struck, but I didn't know that then.) A bluish orange flame burst up. In the little light it made, I thought I saw the Devil, leaning against the curved viaduct wall. For a second I saw his face. The match light made his eyebrows seem to slant weirdly, devilishly up.

Then the flame died. The dark seemed even darker.

Help, someone help me! I tried to scream. No sound came out of my mouth. And the other thing I thought only happened in stories also happened to me: I couldn't move. My feet and legs felt turned to stone.

"Come over here, little girl," said the "Devil" into the silence. He sounded ordinary, Viennese. But I wasn't fooled. I thought, That's just how the Devil would sound.

"Want some *Kaugummi*?"

I knew what that was: peppermint on the outside, something like rubber inside. Like candy. But you didn't swallow it, you only chewed it. For hours, as long as you liked. Then you spit it out. They don't make it here in Austria. It's imported from America.

"You'd like some, wouldn't you?" He moved away from the wall and came near me. I stood there like a statue. He reached for my hand and put a little piece of something in it. Then came the noise again, *Krrrtttzzz*. This time I saw him strike the match. Another flame burst up. "Look."

His pants were unbuttoned, and a stick or something stuck

straight out from there. I don't know why I wrote "or something." I know what it was. I knew then too.

He reached for my other hand. I knew what he wanted to make me do: Touch him there.

Well, my legs changed from stone, I could run, and I did, fast as a greyhound—I'd never run so fast in my life—toward the other side, where light came streaming in. Let me get out, I implored with every footfall, every breath.

I reached the other side. The sunshine dazzled me, it looked like Heaven.

And who, of all the almost one million people in Vienna, should come along just then but Lieselotte. Walking with her was a boy, taller than she was, who looked just like her, with the same color blondish brown hair, the same light-green eyes, and a pointy nose and jutting out chin with a little cleft in the middle. Her brother, Heinz. She'd told me about him. They lived right near there, so meeting them wasn't such a miracle. But it felt like one to me.

"*Heh,* what's the matter with you?" Heinz asked.

I must still have looked scared. I pointed to the viaduct.

"Oh," said Lieselotte with a look that told me she already knew, I didn't have to tell. So then I realized I was not the only person in the world to whom such a thing had happened! I felt so enormously relieved, I laughed and threw my arms around her, the way little children do. And if we hadn't already been friends, we'd have become friends then and there.

"Did old Kaugummi Karl open his pants? Did he show you his *Schwanz*?" asked Heinz.

Lieselotte shoved him. "Don't talk like that!"

"Why not? That's what he does! Did he give you *Kaugummi*?"

I opened my hand. The piece was so small, I couldn't break it in three, so I bit it in three and gave them each one.

They walked me back through the viaduct. Lieselotte and I held our noses. "*Heh*, Kaugummi Karl, where are you?" Heinz yelled at the top of his lungs. But Kaugummi Karl was gone.

Kaethe only now came out of the store. All she had bought was six decca bologna! The rest of the time she must have spent in the back room, cuddling with Herr Wegner. He has a big bald spot and a nose shaped like a lightbulb and fat fingers with hair growing out of the knuckles. I don't see how Kaethe could have liked him, but she did.

She didn't guess, or even care, where I'd been.

Lieselotte came home to play with me that afternoon. I don't remember what we played, probably school with my dolls, and Black Cat and lotto. I do remember that we talked a lot and told each other secrets and had the wonderful feeling you get at that age when you know you can say anything and the other person will listen and won't laugh at you.

I still remember what she wore the Thursday we became friends: a blue and white plaid dress with a round lace collar, hand-crocheted. And blue bows at the ends of her braids. It was during recess, and we were outside in the school yard. She had taken a piece of chalk from the blackboard and was drawing Heaven and Hell boxes on the ground. "Look out," I said, tapping her on the shoulder, "here comes Frau Sommert."

"We mustn't mark up the pavement," said Frau Sommert, and took away the chalk.

I know it was a Thursday because right after recess we had Religious Instruction—for the first time.

"Catholic girls, line up in alphabetical order," Frau Sommert commanded. "Jewish girls, behind them, in alphabetical order too."

Not everybody knew the alphabet yet, so this took a while.

Finally the line was formed. It so happened there were no Catholic girls in our class whose names started with *W, X, Y,* or *Z.* Therefore Lieselotte Vessely was last in the Catholic line.

It also happened that no Jewish girls (six in all) had names starting with *A, B,* or *C. D,* Dornenwald, came first.

Juch-heh! I could stand right behind Lieselotte. And I wished, I wished I could go to the same room as she.

Suddenly I felt I could. . . .

Of course I knew perfectly well that children can't change their religion. It's against the law. You either have to be baptized as a baby or have to wait till you're grown up. Yes, but look where I stood in line! What if God had arranged this as a special favor? What if He was making an exception, giving me this chance?

I went with the Catholic girls.

"The teacher is my uncle Ludwig," Lieselotte whispered to me in the hall. That made me want to go with them even more.

Uncle Ludwig is a priest. He had on a long black dress down to the floor—a cassock, but I didn't know that word yet. He had silver-rimmed glasses, wavy hair, and a friendly face.

When the twenty-three Catholic girls and I were seated, he held his arms out and spread his hands, like a make-believe roof over all our heads. He said, "God bless you." I felt as though God had already blessed me very much.

Then he called the roll. Of course, I was not on it.

He came over to where I sat, next to Lieselotte. He crouched down so his face was level with mine and asked, "What's your name, little one?"

"Inge Dornenwald."

Lieselotte poked me and whispered, "Say 'Father.'" I opened my mouth to. But I couldn't, to someone who wasn't. I guess that told him louder than my name not being on the roll that I'd come to the wrong room.

So much for God's special arrangement. . . .

Father Ludwig didn't get mad. He told the class to sit quietly while he took me to the right room.

On the way there we met the other religion teacher, Frau Schönvogel. She'd come out to look for me.

"Here's your missing one." Father Ludwig handed me over. "God greet you, Inge."

I wanted so much to say "God greet you" back to him! But then I thought he'd wonder which God I meant, and if he asked, what would I say? So I said nothing and looked down at the floor, ashamed of what he must be thinking: that I was badly brought up and didn't have manners.

Frau Schönvogel led me into her classroom.

Hedi Stein and Elfriede Kaplan laughed, "Tee hee."

"No, girls. We mustn't laugh at Inge for getting lost. It's sad.

We should feel sorry when a child from a Jewish home doesn't know where she belongs. Tell me, Inge, do you go to temple?"

I'd only gone once, the week before school began. My father had taken me, perhaps because he'd foreseen the question. "Yes, Frau Schönvogel," I answered.

"Can you explain how you happened to wander into Father Ludwig's class?"

My cheeks got hot. "I, um, made a mistake."

"Well, I'm sure you won't make it again. Now sit down. There, next to Elfriede."

Then she drew the first two letters of the Hebrew alphabet, aleph and bet, on the blackboard. We copied them into our notebooks and practice-wrote them, two lines each.

Then we talked about holidays. She asked who liked which one the best. Chanukah, said everybody.

Then she asked, with a come-on-tell-me smile, "How many of you have Christmas trees at that time of year?"

I and one other girl fell into the trap and raised our hands. "We always have a beautiful orange and blue and silver and golden bird on top," I said proudly.

"Do you!" She pointed a finger at me. "That's very wrong. This year I want you to be sure and tell your parents not to have a Christmas tree."

"But we have a menorah too," I said, on the verge of crying.

"That's no excuse," said Frau Schönvogel.

When I told my mother, she lit a fresh cigarette from the one she was just stubbing out. "Never mind, Ingelein." Then she exploded, "How does that woman dare stick her nose into what we do?"

"Hannerl, Hannerl," said my father, and then the sentence in French that means "Don't talk in front of the child."

They talked about it later that night when I was in bed. (My room is right next to the living room. We eat in there too, and my parents sit there evenings when they are alone, or when there's company. My bed is right against the wall. The wall is not too thick, so I can hear what they say.)

Of course I don't remember exactly anymore. But Mutti was angry, not just at Frau Schönvogel, but at schools' insisting on religion. She said that's meddling with how parents bring their children up. She wished they could bring me up without any such "nonsense."

Vati said yes, but it didn't matter so much, it wouldn't do me any harm, just as it hadn't harmed them in their school days, and she shouldn't let it upset her so.

Then they went out, to the Schottentor. That is the coffee-house where they always meet their friends.

Next day at school Lieselotte said, "Guess what my uncle Ludwig said."

Something embarrassing about my "mistake" yesterday, I was sure.

"He said you're nice, and he's glad he met you."

So for the next few Thursdays I hung around his classroom before and after recess, hoping to catch glimpses of him. And when I did, I gave him shy smiles, and once I even got out, "*Grüss Gott* (God greet you), Father Ludwig."

He greeted me back, by my name, he remembered! And he didn't ask which God I meant.

So then for a while when I prayed at night, "Now I lay me," God in my prayers wore a long black cassock and had silver-rimmed glasses and wavy hair.

Heh, it's light outside! It's starting to snow!

Friday afternoon, February 11

Snow came down like powdered sugar out of Mitzi's sugar sprinkler when she bakes.

On such mornings, making fresh tracks on the sidewalks on our way to school, Lieselotte and I would sometimes pretend to be famous explorers finding buried civilizations. Once we found a whole subcontinent: Ancient East Diefenland, an even more important discovery than Troy. Then we took turns being the King of Sweden and awarding each other the Nobel Prize. I tried to get into that kind of mood this morning. But I couldn't, by myself.

When I got to Herrengasse Gymnasium, it was only twenty to eight. The doors were still locked.

So I walked the short way over to the Stefansplatz. I love it there, especially early in the morning, when it's still not crowded. I walked along the southwest wall of St. Stephen's Cathedral, where the three gargoyles are, not too high up, so you can see their faces. Snowflakes stuck to their ears and bristly eyebrows and fell into their ferocious grins. They were put there for the purpose of keeping evil spirits away. When I was little, I used to wonder how they did that.

I let snowflakes settle on *my* eyebrows and caught some on my tongue as I stood there craning my neck, looking up at old

"Steffl." (I'm not really on intimate enough terms with it to call it by its nickname, but lots of people do.)

The top seemed to wobble in the sky. But that was only because I stood so near.

I walked around to the far side, where the other tower was begun. That one only reaches as high as the roof. I tried to imagine how St. Stephen's would look if they had finished it, if there were twin towers, not just one.

In the stillness of the morning I could almost hear me and Lieselotte scaring Mitzi with that story. . . .

We were nine. It was a warm afternoon, we had no coats on. Lieselotte wore a pleated skirt with a real waistline and no babyish straps over the shoulders like mine. Her hair was loose. It flowed down her back in crinkly waves. How I envied and admired it!

Mitzi had just started working for us. (Kaethe had left, but not to marry Herr Wegner. To everyone's surprise he already had a wife.) Mitzi comes from Mondsee, the place where we spend summers. She still looked very countryish and wore a dirndl, and her hair in thick braids twisted like two big garden snails around her ears.

In those days when I was still in elementary school, I wasn't allowed to go places by myself or with just a friend. The maid was supposed to take me—and a friend if I wanted—on afternoon walks. That meant to the Stadtpark or the Prater or along the Danube Canal, anywhere with "fresh air." Not to the Inner City, with its narrow streets and traffic. But Mitzi didn't know that yet. And we didn't tell her.

"Yessas, Maria!" she gasped when we got near St. Stephen's. "That tower's so high it's shaking back and forth in the clouds! It's a wonder it doesn't come crashing down on our heads!"

Lieselotte and I exchanged looks.

I said, "It could, someday."

"Holy saints preserve us! You're joking, aren't you?"

"No, I'm not."

"It really could," said Lieselotte.

We took Mitzi by the hands and led her to the place where I stood this morning.

I said, "Look up there! About five hundred years ago they started building this new tower. They wanted it to look just like the other one and be just as high. Then a frightful thing happened."

"What?"

I started from the beginning, the way we'd learned it in school: "In the Middle Ages there lived a builder named Hans Puchsbaum. He bragged that he could build a second tower in less time and for less money than any other builder. So the burgomaster said, 'Build it, then,' and promised him good pay. First everything went fine. But then he ran out of stones. And he couldn't get enough workmen either. It looked as if he wouldn't finish as fast as he'd said, or ever. He didn't know what to do. And then . . . You tell it from here, Lieselotte."

Lieselotte made her voice low and spooky. "A stranger appeared. He wore a green vest. He dragged one foot behind him like somebody lame. He carried a cane. Only it looked like a pitchfork. And do you know what grew out of his head?"

"What?" Mitzi's eyes got round, like a little girl's.

Lieselotte and I, as though we'd rehearsed this, put our fingers to our heads and pointed up. Our faces stayed unsmiling. "Horns!"

Mitzi crossed herself. She drew her breath in through her teeth. *"Yessas, Maria 'nd Yosef!"*

"Shh! Don't say that!" Lieselotte warned her and continued: "The stranger asked Hans Puchsbaum, 'Would you like me to help? I can finish that tower in no time.'

"Hans Puchsbaum hesitated. He had an idea who the stranger might be. He asked, 'What do you want in return?'

"'Oh, nothing much. Just that you don't utter the names of God or the Virgin till the tower is done.'

"That didn't sound too hard. Hans Puchsbaum agreed. Everything went fine. Everybody was amazed how fast the tower got higher and higher. Then one day Hans Puchsbaum was standing up there on the scaffolding, and he saw the girl he was going to marry, down below. Maybe right where we are standing. He hadn't seen her for a long time because he'd been so busy. Well, he got excited, and he yelled to her, 'Maria!' That was her name."

"It's my real name too," Mitzi whispered, looking really scared.

I said, "We won't tell you the rest if you don't want us to."

"No, you can't stop there!"

I felt a little ashamed of ourselves. But it was so much fun, and it made me feel so really, truly best friends with Lieselotte, as though the differences between us didn't matter, and I wished that feeling could go on and on.

"As soon as Hans Puchsbaum shouted 'Maria,' there came a thunderclap, terribly loud," we continued, like a chorus.

"You finish, Inge," Lieselotte said.

"All right. Then another thunderclap, louder than an earthquake. And the scaffolding came crashing down. So did the tower. So did Hans Puchsbaum. And guess what: They couldn't find his body anywhere. It vanished without a trace. But a huge, gigantic shape with a green vest and horns was seen hovering over the shambles. Lots of people saw it. Some said they heard horrible hellish laughter. And nobody tried finishing the tower ever again after that."

Mitzi clutched our hands. "Let's go home!"

"Don't you want to go inside? It's beautiful in there," said Lieselotte.

"Yes, but what about . . . ?" Mitzi looked at me.

I knew what she was thinking. I said, "Don't worry, I'm allowed in. They let Jews into churches."

"That's true," Lieselotte assured her.

"Oh. Well, I didn't know. I never knew a—"

A Jew before, she'd nearly said. She blushed and looked embarrassed.

I said, "That's all right." And we went into St. Stephen's.

This morning I didn't go inside. I didn't want to remember that part of it. I headed over toward school.

But I remembered anyway. The memory wouldn't, and still won't, leave me alone. It makes me ashamed, but it's part of my real and true feelings. So it belongs in here:

The three of us went through the portal. Mitzi whispered, "It's tremendous!"

21

I breathed in the smell. It smelled of hundreds and hundreds of years of candle flames, stone, incense, and quiet, mixed with cool, dank air. By the entrance stands a dark pink marble basin on a marble column, like a bird bath. It's for holy water. Lieselotte and Mitzi dipped their hands in there—very slowly, I thought. Why were they taking so long? But it only seemed long to me because I felt left out. I wished like anything that I could dip my hand in too.

They crossed themselves with wet fingers and bobbed down on one knee.

Then we walked down the aisle and all around and showed Mitzi the tombs and altars and pictures and statues. She kneeled in front of an old wooden statue of the Virgin called "The Servants' Madonna." She prayed to it as though it were there especially for her. By the time she was done, all the fright was gone from her face.

Now comes the part I feel awful about, to this day. I've thought and thought about it, and I still can't understand it. This morning, heading for school, I tried not to think about it, all over again. I tried to distract myself: I counted cracks under the snow in the sidewalk and stepped on every third crack. I looked into shop windows. I noticed people's boot prints and dogs' pawprints in the snow. A lady in a curly black fur coat came by with a little curly black dog on a red-lacquered leash, wearing a fashionable red and white dog coat. I thought how Lieselotte would have laughed at the dog's outfit, and I smiled. But then I caught my reflection in a shop window and saw how forced my smile looked. The distractions weren't working. The only thing really on my mind was, What had come over me and Lieselotte in St. Stephen's that day?

The sidewalk was clear of passersby, no one would see. So I stuck my thumbs in my ears, wiggled my fingers, opened my mouth wide, made a face like a gargoyle at my reflection in the window. It was stupid, I know. But I hoped it might drive the memory away. . . .

What had started us off was seeing a lady wearing a lilac hat with a bird with real feathers perched on top, a tight skirt, and very-high-heeled shoes. She knelt in front of an altar, praying, but not with her hands folded. One hand was busy scratching her behind. Her fingernails grated against the cloth of her skirt. I don't know who let out the first giggle, me or Lieselotte. I just remember the two of us laughing, harder and harder, we couldn't help it, it made our insides hurt, it stopped being fun. I clamped my lips shut, but laughter burst through. We put our hands over our mouths, then over each other's. It didn't help. I felt like I was on the roller coaster in the Wurstelprater, wishing it would stop but hurtling on and on.

Mitzi shushed us. A church servant in a long black coat came striding over, looking mad. He shushed us really loud. Mitzi made a curtsy down to the floor and begged his pardon for us in her country accent. And we still couldn't stop.

She pushed us to the nearest door. Getting to it took forever. People shook their heads as we passed, wondering what possessed us. I remember thinking, What if we never reach the door? What if we spend eternity not getting there, and everyone keeps staring? What if this already is eternity, and we're in hell but don't know it?

We did get to the door at last, and out.

"You made me so ashamed, I hoped the floor would open up and you'd fall in and never be heard from again!" said Mitzi.

When she got over being mad, she asked Lieselotte, "Will you be confirmed in there?"

"Yes."

And they talked about that: whether Lieselotte's confirmation dress would be of tulle or voile; how long her veil should be; which would be prettier, white kid-leather or black patent shoes; what kind of flower decorations should be on the fiacre in which she would ride through the Prater afterward; what color the horse should be; and how many people could comfortably sit in the fiacre with her.

Then Mitzi asked me, "Don't Jewish children also get confirmed?"

"I don't think so. Boys have *bar mitzvah,* but that's different."

"That's a shame," said Mitzi.

"I'm inviting you to my confirmation," said Lieselotte. "You'll sit next to me in the fiacre."

As it turned out, she couldn't invite me. Her father wouldn't hear of it. Anyway, by then my parents were already against our friendship and wouldn't have wanted me to go.

All the way in the back of my wardrobe, behind boots and skates and cartons of put-away clothes, I keep a box marked PRIVATE, DO NOT TOUCH.

I wrote a story on the day of our laughter attack in St. Stephen's to try to make myself feel better, and I've kept it in that box. I just took it out so I could put it into here. Of course by then I didn't really believe in the Devil anymore, at least not in the way I used to. He just seemed to come in handy for the story:

Once or twice a century the Devil is invited up to heaven for a visit. And if God is in a good mood, He grants him a favor.

Well, on his last visit the Devil said, "Dear God, in Vienna there is a cathedral. It's called St. Stephen's. You know it well."

"So do you," said God reproachfully. He was thinking of the second tower that never got finished.

The Devil tried to look ashamed. "Yes, I know it, but only from the outside. I've heard the inside is still more beautiful. Dear God, won't you let me go in there, just one time?"

"Absolutely not. It's against the rules," said God.

"But please, please," the Devil begged, "make an exception, just once."

God started to relent. "All right, just once. Go on in. But only as far as the vestry. Not one step farther."

That wasn't enough for the Devil. "Suppose," he began, "somebody comes in who does not touch the, um, er, oh, you know, the, um, water—"

"You mean the holy water," God said.

"Yes. And suppose that somebody also does not,

um, er—" (Certain words are hard for the Devil to say.)

"Cross himself," said God.

"Yes. Thank you. Or herself. Dear God, would you allow me to follow that somebody farther in and see the sights?"

"Oh, all right," God gave in. "Only promise you'll do no harm."

"On my grandmother's whiskers, I swear it! Thank you, thank you a lot, dear God!" said the Devil.

And he plunged straight down to the Stefansplatz. He made himself invisible and went into St. Stephen's. He waited and waited inside the door till finally somebody came in who did not touch the holy water and did not cross herself.

"*Juch-heh*," said the Devil, and followed her around. And either he had no grandmother or his grandmother had no whiskers, because he did do harm, this much: He tickled the girl's funny bone (which people think is near the elbow but is actually somewhere else, only the Devil knows where). And she laughed and laughed and couldn't stop, and so did her friend, who was with her.

I couldn't think of an ending. I couldn't decide (I still can't) how angry God would have been, and whether and how the Devil would have been punished.

What else there is inside my PRIVATE, DO NOT TOUCH box:

Other things I've written.

A baby tooth of mine.

One forget-me-not earring from the pair Kaethe gave me when she left. (The second one is lost.)

My old flannel elephant, Schnurli Wurli.

Some photographs of my parents skiing. Some of me as a baby. One of Lieselotte and me at my seventh birthday party. One of my mother as a young girl, and one of her as a baby sitting on Grandmother Ida's lap.

An edelweiss (pressed) that my father found on a mountain.

The picture postcard of the dachshund sent from Regensburg in December with my address in block letters and nothing written on it.

My one letter, with B.S.L., from Lieselotte.

I'll put the letter into this book. But first I'll explain where B.S.L. comes from:

One day when we were ten, we were at Lieselotte's in the kitchen with her *Mutterl*. (I used to love how that word sounds, warmer and cozier than "Mutti," I thought.) Anyway, she was making meat dumplings, and she let us help. A kettle of broth simmered on the stove. She told about when she was our age, on a farm near Linz, helping *her* mother make dumplings just like these. After every dumpling we shaped, Lieselotte and I popped bits of the meat—smoked butt, delicious—into our mouths.

Finally Frau Vessely gave us both smacks (not hard ones) and said, "That's what my *Mutterl* would have given *me*!"

I was thinking how at home I felt, and I caught myself wishing I really were in their family.

When the dumplings were simmering in the broth, Frau Vessely went to take an afternoon nap.

"Now let's drink blood brotherhood," said Lieselotte.

I'd never heard of that. But I wanted to.

She took down a bottle of cooking wine. She poured a little into a glass. "We need a needle." She went and got one. "Now we prick our fingers."

"How do you know?"

"I read about it, in a book Heinz has. Want to be first?"

"No, you."

She stuck the needle in her finger. She didn't even wince. She squeezed two drops of her blood into the wine.

I pricked my finger. I didn't wince either. I squeezed my blood in.

We stirred up the wine with the blood.

"Now we link arms." Lieselotte lifted the glass. "Now we drink blood brotherhood."

"Shouldn't it be blood *sister*hood?"

"I don't know. Heinz says there's no such thing. But you're right. If we drink blood sisterhood, then there will be such a thing. Let's."

Lieselotte drank first. Then I. It tasted sweet with just a trace of bitter. It burned going down our throats: It felt warm inside our stomachs.

When we were done, we still had our arms linked, so we swung each other around. I bumped against the table, she against the sink.

"We're drunk!"

"That wine is strong!"

I can still feel how the warmth spread through me. "Blood sisters forever!" said Lieselotte.

"And ever," I said.

"And if we ever need each other, we'll be there."

B.S.L. stands for Blood-Sisterly Love.

But now she's gone, and I don't even have her address. Here follows the one letter Lieselotte wrote to me three months ago:

> Munich
> Tuesday, November 9, 1937
>
> Dear Inge,
>
> It's only two days since I saw you, and already I miss you a lot.
>
> The trip went fast, no wonder: Herr Hartmann drove sixty kilometers an hour, even in the mountains, around curves. Mutterl held her hand in front of her mouth a lot of the time. At the border Herr Hartmann showed the guard something in his wallet, and the guard let us through ahead of the other cars.
>
> The place Papa found us to live is very nice. It's

near a park and near the River Isar. We have the whole upstairs of a two-story house. It has a garden in the back, and we're allowed to use it. It would be perfect for a dog if we ever get one. I was afraid I might have to share a room with Heinz, but I have my own.

Aunt Louisa (Papa's sister), Uncle Poldi, and my cousins, Helga and Heidi, were here when we arrived. Helga brought me a skirt she has outgrown that I can use for Jungmädel (the youth group girls our age are in). Aunt Louisa had supper all ready. Papa hugged and kissed us a lot. He wore his Storm Trooper's uniform even though it was Sunday, because it was such a special occasion. He opened a special bottle of schnapps. And everybody except Heidi (she's only seven) drank to our new life. Have you ever gulped down fire? That's what schnapps tastes like.

I haven't seen much of Munich yet, only the Marienplatz, which is in the middle, like the Stefansplatz in Vienna, and the Isar, and the streets between our house and my new school.

Heinz loves it here. He already has friends and acts as if he owns the place.

I already have an enemy: Edeltraut Wiecks. She is a skinny beanpole (much, much skinnier than you!) with Shirley Temple curls and two faces: one, sweet and kind, for when the teacher is watching;

the other, spiteful and snide, when the teacher turns her back. Our homeroom teacher, Fräulein Schmidt, appointed her to be my "guide" and "helper" till I get used to things. Here's how she "guides" and "helps" me: She sticks to me like a leech; sits next to me in all our classes; jumps, kicks, bends, and stretches beside me in calisthenics (mornings *and* afternoons!); pokes me in the ribs when I forget to give the greeting (more about that later); and says things like, "You Austrians are sloppy weaklings."

This school is called Scholz-Klink High School for German Girls, after Frau Gertrude Scholz-Klink. I think she is still alive. She founded the German Women's League (that's just like the Bund Deutscher Mädel, but for grown-ups). She made up the motto: *Although our weapon is only the soup ladle, its might must be as great as that of other weapons.* This motto is carved into the wall of the auditorium above the stage. Every Scholz-Klink girl has to know it by heart.

This school is quite a change after Herrengasse Gymnasium. For instance, here we don't have Latin, Geography, or Natural Science. We do have five hours of physical training a day: two and a half of calisthenics, two and a half of games. And all my muscles are sore, even in parts of me I never knew had muscles! But at least in volleyball today I made three spectacular points in a row (excuse the bragging). I did it less for our team than to make Edeltraut admit, "Not bad, for an Austrian."

We also don't have French or English or Ancient History. On the other hand, we have Housewifely Arts—to learn to wield the ladle! And we have Racial Science with a Herr Professor Wandke, who, except for being bald, looks more like a hedgehog than any human I ever saw. Today we measured one another's heads from tops to chins and memorized the names of different "Germanic racial facial types."

We also have Herr Professor Wandke for History. In History we are studying the Munich parts of *Mein Krampf*—oops, look how I spelled that! Probably because my belly aches. Whose wouldn't, after so much calisthenics?

One strange thing about this school: Although everything else is strictly compulsory, Religious Instruction is optional! All you need, to get out of it, is one parent's signature on a form.

Papa was glad to sign it. He signed Heinz's form too. Mutterl said—as I knew she would!—"Oh, goodness me, what would Uncle Ludwig say?"

"That Religious Instruction is like semolina pudding without cinnamon or chocolate in the middle, the way most priests teach it," I said. It's true, he does think that.

"Lieselotte, don't blaspheme," said Mutterl.

"Rosi, don't make such a mountain out of a mole-hill," said Papa. He patted her on the head and winked at Heinz and me, to let us know how "typically womanish" she was being.

I may not hand my form in. I don't know yet.

More about the greeting: Remember my old wooden *Hampelmann,* with the arms and legs that moved when you pulled his string? That's how my arm feels! You have to stick it out with every greeting, and you give the greeting all the time! For instance, yesterday morning, just between seven thirty and eight fifteen, I gave it a total of thirteen times. Here's a list of everyone to whom I said it:

1• To Herr Pfaltz. (He, his wife, and their two children live downstairs. I minded the children, Rudi and Uta, yesterday afternoon while Frau Pfaltz went shopping.)

2• To the postman on our street (speaking of whom, write SOON!).

3• To the policeman at the corner.

4• Then we met a friend of Papa's, also in SA uniform, so we greeted him. (I forgot to mention, Papa was walking me partway to school.)

5• Then came an SS man, and we greeted him, even though Papa didn't know him. That doesn't matter. Papa says all people in uniform greet one another.

6• Then Papa wanted me to greet *him* like that! Instead of saying *Tschüss*. He says I should unlearn that, people don't say it here.

7• When I was walking by myself so I wouldn't get out of practice, I greeted some sparrows in the gutter. They were hopping around, inspecting fresh horse droppings. They didn't greet me back, ha ha.

8• Inside the school I forgot to greet the girl whom I asked how to get to the Frau Direktor's office. She said I had to, so I did.

9• Then I greeted the Frau Direktor's secretary, Fräulein Pfitzner.

10• Then I greeted the Frau Direktor. Her name is Seidlmeier. She is a noble-looking woman, tall and broad, with a bosom like two volleyballs and steel-gray hair, braided into a crown on top of her head. She looks like a queen. But she smelled of cabbage salad. Imagine eating that for breakfast!

11• I greeted her again on my way out of there.

12• In my new homeroom, Fräulein Schmidt.

13• Then in the gym, at the start of calisthenics, I and the entire student body, in gym shoes, black shorts, and white shirts, our right arms high in the air, thundered out to the calisthenics teacher, *Heil* You-know-who! By then it was eight fifteen.

By the end of the morning I felt like a phonograph record with a crack in it. Or a parrot who knows only those two words.

But guess what happened as I was going home for noon meal (by my lonely self, while everyone else walked in bunches): I saw a dachshund puppy, all frisky and sniffing everything. Well, you know how I get. I rushed to him and petted him. And the lady who was walking him said *"Grüss Gott"* to me, just like in Vienna!

The puppy's name is Schnackerl. He's five months old, and he's the color of chestnuts. I fell in love with him.

I forgot to tell you one good thing about Scholz-Klink: It's closed on Wednesdays. All German schools are. Wednesdays everybody goes on hikes and outings.

Now I have to stop, because I have to go downstairs and mind Uta and Rudi again so Herr and Frau Pfaltz can come up for coffee and cake with my parents.

Inge, give my best regards to Susi König, Anni Hopf, Fräulein Pappenheim, Mitzi, Fredl, Upstairs-Evi, and whoever else you think would want them. And write immediately! I'll count the seconds till I hear from you. My address is on the envelope.

Much B.S.L.,
Your Lieselotte

I wrote her back immediately: that I was thrilled to get her letter. How long the time seemed since she left. That a new girl, Ilse

Holtzer, sat next to me at Lieselotte's old desk, and I couldn't like her, though she seemed quite nice.

I enclosed a kick in the pants to Edeltraut Wiecks and regards to Herr Professor Hedgehog.

I wrote two bits of Herrengasse Gymnasium gossip: that Susi König will get suspended next time she's caught smoking in the toilet; and that Anni Hopf has a "flirt," or so she claims.

I wrote that the Löwbergs had been here for supper the night before; that Tommi deigned to play checkers with me, and when I won, he pretended he'd let me!

I wrote that I'd finished *Beneath Distant Skies,* all 397 pages, corny but thrilling, and was starting to read *Leatherstocking,* also long and about Indians, but hard to get into.

I thanked her for being so tactful, writing "You-know-who" instead of Hitler's name, but she didn't have to, I was really not scared of him.

Hitler has to leave hands strictly off Austria. One false move and Mussolini would come to our rescue. My father had said so to the Löwbergs the night before I wrote this letter.

"Your word in God's ear," Aunt Marianne had said.

"Teu, teu, teu," Uncle Herbert had said, and knocked three times on wood—that's a joking thing one does to keep the Devil away.

I asked Lieselotte in my letter if there was the slightest chance she might ever move back to Vienna. (I'd already dreamed twice that she had.)

I sent regards to Heinz. I confided that although he usually either teased or ignored me, I missed him, and that when we were little, I sometimes pretended he was *my* older brother too.

I sent best regards to her mother. (None to her father; I didn't think he'd want any from me.) I asked how it was now that her father had more time to spend at home with them.

I complained about having a lot of Latin homework (to make her feel better that they don't teach it at her school).

I wrote that I'd count the seconds till her next letter, and of course sent B.S.L.

"Fräulein Lieselotte Vessely," I wrote on the envelope. Then I looked on the back of hers, to copy the address. But it was crossed out in thick black ink! Not a single letter or number of it showed through!

I threw my coat on and called to Mitzi, "I have to go someplace, I'll be back soon."

"Where, in this lousy weather?"

"I'll tell you later."

"Well, put your galoshes on and take an umbrella."

"I'm not made of sugar, I won't melt!" And I went, running most of the way.

When I got to their old house, I stood a moment, shook the rain off, and caught my breath. Then I rang the bell for the janitor, Herr Magrutsch.

Let him not be drunk, I hoped. Not that he's so nice when he's sober. Either way, he used to yell at us for playing ball against the side of the house or even just for sitting on the front steps.

He took his time. Finally he came. He swayed, like a rowboat on a stormy lake. "What do you want?" he asked. Then he belched and filled the air between us with beer fumes.

"I, um, was wondering, did the Vesselys by any chance leave a forwarding address?"

He raised his bushy eyebrows toward the ceiling, as if that was a crazy question. "Not with me." He shrugged and started to stagger away, then remembered he'd left the door open, staggered back, and banged it shut in my face.

But I was not defeated. I still had somewhere else to go: Lieselotte's uncle Ludwig's parish church. He'd surely have their address.

I took a streetcar to Siemmering. Even though it's in the Eleventh District, it's not far, only a fifteen-minute ride.

The church, St. Anselm's, is right near the streetcar stop. The outside must have been cleaned recently—it was lighter gray than most churches, almost white. It was small and graceful-looking, with baroque curves at the top. And it didn't seem forbidding. In fact, the door stood open.

I walked past it to the rectory. I rang the bell. While I stood waiting, I summoned back my memory of Father Ludwig's kind face. I imagined him smiling, starting to remember me.

"Don't you touch that door handle!" croaked a hunched-over woman with a face like the witch's in "Hänsel and Gretel." "I worked my fingers raw polishing the brass. What do you want?"

"I'd like to see Father Ludwig, please."

"He's busy now. He's with a parishioner. You can wait if you want, but it may be a while." She looked me up and down. "You're not in this parish, are you?"

"Um, no."

She shook her head as if to say, Then you have no business taking his time, or mine.

I said, "Excuse me." I put my coat collar up and started walking to the streetcar stop.

"Just a minute," she called after me in her croaky voice. "Who shall I say . . . ?"

But I'd lost my courage. I called, "Thank you, never mind," and ran, because a streetcar was coming.

On the streetcar going home I wracked my brain. How was I going to get my letter to Lieselotte? Finally I got an idea. It turned out pretty badly. . . .

One day when we were nine years old, Lieselotte said to me, "Guess where I went with my father."

The Vesselys had just come back from visiting their relatives in Munich.

"Where?" I asked her.

"To the Brown House. Isn't that a funny name for a building?"

"Yes. Does it have *Lebkuchen* walls and a chocolate chimney?" I was joking, I didn't really think it had.

"No! It's just a big building with offices inside. My father knows people who work there. He might work there too one day if we move to Munich."

"Oh, please don't move away," I'd said. . . .

My idea was, maybe now he did work there.

So when I got home, I addressed my letter, like this:

Fräulein Lieselotte Vessely
c/o Herr Georg Vessely
The Brown House
Munich
Bavaria
Germany

I licked it closed and went into the study for stamps.

To my surprise my father was sitting there at his desk. He'd come home while I was out. And when I came back, I must have been so preoccupied, I didn't notice his coat on the coatrack in the hall. Or else his coat had gotten so wet, Mitzi had hung it in the bathroom.

"*Servus,* Ingelein." He stood up and kissed me hello. He saw the envelope in my hand. "Do you need stamps for that?"

"Yes. For abroad."

"Oh? To whom are you writing?"

I didn't say.

He frowned. He reached for the envelope, read the address. "I can't believe what I see!" He ripped it in half and then into little shreds. The shreds looked very white compared to how red his face was turning. The vein in his forehead stood out and throbbed. He took me by the shoulders and shook me like an apple tree.

He's not that kind of man, really. He is always—well, almost always—very calm and self-controlled.

He only got this mad at me one other time. I was seven. We were at Oma Sofie's. She's my father's mother. I'm never at my best when we go to visit there. It's full of breakable knickknacks you are not supposed to touch or even go near. And I used to be afraid of Usch. Usch is Oma Sofie's housekeeper. Her name is really Ursula. But my father and his older brother, Richard (who died in the World War), and Aunt Emmi couldn't say that when they were small, so they called her Usch, and it stuck.

One time when I was little, I had to sleep over there, and accidentally I wet the bed. Well, she called me a baby and made me feel even worse about it than I would have anyway. And she kept reminding me of it. Even now she still sometimes brings it up. Now, of course, I'm not afraid of her anymore. But I used to be. I used to feel sorry for my father and Aunt Emmi, having to be around her all the time when they were children. But Vati says she can be nice too, and she means well. He's pretty fond of her. And Oma Sofie adores her and always says she would be lost without her.

Anyway, Aunt Emmi, Uncle Hugo, and Cousin Madeleine from Switzerland were there on a visit. Madeleine was only four. Usch had given me the job of keeping Madeleine entertained in the parlor so the grown-ups could have coffee (out of Oma Sofie's beautiful blue and gold demitasse service) in the dining room in peace and quiet.

I told Madeleine a wonderful story about how she was a noble princess with royal blood flowing in her veins and that she had been adopted as a tiny baby. Well, the next thing I knew she went dashing in to the grown-ups and yelled to Aunt Emmi, "Mama, Mama, did I really come out of somebody else's belly?"

Aunt Emmi let her demitasse fall on the floor. It broke.

My father leaped up from the table. "Inge, come here!" And he grabbed me and shook me till I was reeling.

It was true! Not the princess part. But that Madeleine was adopted.

Oma Sofie was so upset, she got a headache and had to take Pyramidon tablets and lie down in her bedroom with the shades pulled.

"You're a wicked girl," said Usch. She was sure, she still is to this day, that I'd known about Madeleine's adoption all along.

Vati believed me that I hadn't. And later he said he was sorry that he'd lost his temper so.

"Inge, Inge," he said, slowly starting to quiet down, the afternoon of the letter. And he told me he was sorry for shaking me so hard.

I said, "That letter was important."

He took my face between his hands. His hands felt gentle. He has the most sky-blue eyes of anyone I know.

He looked at me lovingly, and I could love him again. "Ingelein, have you any idea what the Brown House is?"

"An office building."

"It's Nazi Party Headquarters," said my father. "Now do you understand why I got so angry?"

———

I wrote the letter again. It was still all in my head. I knew how I'd address it—of course, of course, why hadn't I thought of that in the first place?

> Fräulein Lieselotte Vessely, Student
> c/o Scholz-Klink High School for German Girls
> Munich
> Bavaria
> Germany

And I sent it off.

Saturday, February 12

Yesterday as I was finishing writing in here, Upstairs-Evi Fried came down. She's ten and acts even younger than that. She has naturally curly black hair and is shaped like a dumpling. She still goes to my old school in the Löwengasse and may go to Herrengasse Gymnasium next year if she passes the exam.

Anyway, she wanted to play Heaven and Hell. She always does, she's at that age.

"All right." I got my coat. I checked to see if Lieselotte's lucky pebble was in the pocket. It was.

We went down to the courtyard.

The little bit of snow had melted. The ground was dry enough. Evi had chalk and drew the boxes.

Heaven is where you rest. Hell is when you miss. . . .

Lieselotte never used to miss, except if a dog came anywhere near. Then her pebble would land in the wrong box, or she'd lose her balance, almost on purpose, so she could go pet it.

Personally I don't like dogs that much. Especially German shepherds. One time in the country when I was riding a bicycle, one ran after me and bit me in the leg. I got so scared, I threw myself off. I still have a scar on my left knee, not from the bite, from the fall. At least here in the city, dogs like that have to wear muzzles.

With no dogs to distract her, if there were such a thing as the Viennese Heaven and Hell Championship, Lieselotte could definitely have won it.

In the Stadtpark one afternoon I got very mad at myself for playing badly, and she told me her secret: "Pretend nothing else in the whole world exists, just your pebble, the boxes, and you."

I tried, and it helped.

Upstairs-Evi is so little competition, once every few games I let her win.

Afterward I went upstairs with her, and her mother said I should stay for supper. It was cold cuts, all beef. The Frieds are not strictly kosher, but they don't eat meats like ham or bologna. They are much more religious than we are. They go to temple very often and have a mezuzah on their door.

Herr Fried owns a jewelry and watch-repair shop on the Praterstrasse. He said I should come there one of these days, and he'll show me the insides of watches and how they work.

Frau Fried asked me questions about school. She always tries to get me to say how hard it is. Then she says to Evi, "If you were as smart as Inge, we wouldn't have to worry. You'd better study, study, study, or you won't get in." It's nice of Evi not to hate me. If I were she and she were me, I might.

When she was in the first class, she had diphtheria and then had to have her tonsils taken out. That's how she got behind a year.

Diphtheria is a really serious sickness. But Evi says the tonsils were worse because when they put the ether mask on her face, she thought she'd choke to death. Her parents hadn't told her that she was going to have an operation. They'd said they were taking her out for a treat, for ice cream, so she wouldn't get all worried about it in advance. Was she ever surprised! She still has dreams about it, even though it was so long ago.

I've been putting off writing what made my parents want me to stop being friends with Lieselotte:

We were ten. We were just back from summer vacations; me from Mondsee, Lieselotte from near there, but across the German border. We were at her house, comparing mountains we'd climbed to the tops of, lakes we'd swum in, flowers we'd found. She showed me some gentian and alpine roses she was pressing and some photographs of her and Heinz and cousins of theirs on a hike. Also, she taught me a song her cousins had taught her. It went like this:

Raise high the flag,
Close fast and firm the ranks,
SA, march on,

With calm and steadfast tread!
Our comrades who were shot in red-front reaction,
March in spirit side by side with us.

The last two lines got repeated.

"What's 'SA'?" I asked.

"Some sort of soldiers."

"Oh. What's 'red-front reaction'?"

"I don't know. Isn't it a catchy song?"

At ten years old I was really ignorant about world events. (Not that I know so much about the subject even now.) At home my parents didn't—still don't—talk about it in front of me. At school all we learned was patriotic stuff about long ago, how Vienna withstood the Turkish siege, etc. I didn't even know what the World War was about, only that my father fought in it and his brother, Richard (who would have been my uncle), died in it, and that Austria lost, Germany too. Aside from that I knew that Schuschnigg was the chancellor of Austria, and Hitler, of Germany; and that we were lucky to be living here, not there, because Hitler is bad and hates the Jews. Also, I must have known what he looks like from seeing photographs of him in newspapers. Because I recognized him inside a golden frame in Lieselotte's parents' bedroom, on top of a bureau, smiling, holding flowers.

Yes, I thought the song was catchy. The words sounded noble. And the melody stirred up feelings in me I didn't know I could have, such as wanting to march also and being sorry for the "comrades who were shot in red-front reaction," whatever that was. I pictured their shirtfronts getting red with blood.

While Lieselotte was teaching me the song, I made up this scene in my head: I'm in a crowd where Hitler is. Everyone is singing, me included. I'm standing near him. He hears me. "Why, that girl sings beautifully," he says. "Come here, child." I go right up to him. "What is your name?" "Inge Dornenwald." He frowns. "Isn't that a Jewish name?" I say, "Yes," and show him the Jewish star (actually I don't have one) on a chain around my neck. Hitler claps his hand to his forehead and exclaims, "I've been wrong about the Jews!" And from then on he likes Jews and treats them like everybody else—because of me!

That evening I picked out the tune on our piano.

Mutti rushed in. "What are you playing there?"

I played chords to the tune and got ready to smile modestly in case she said, "Ingelein, you're so musical, it's a pity you stopped taking piano lessons."

Instead she put the lid down, nearly on my fingers. "That's a Nazi song!"

My father came in too.

"Inge just played the Horst Wessel song!" said Mutti.

"Where did she learn that?"

"Guess. She spent the afternoon at the Vesselys'."

A long look passed between them.

"Inge, we would rather you didn't spend so much time there," Mutti said.

"Why shouldn't I?"

"Because—well, you see—"

"Because we say so," said my father.

"But Lieselotte is my best friend!"

They didn't say anything to that. But on both their faces was written, Then find another one!

All my life until that moment I had thought of them as unusually intelligent, understanding parents, to be proud of. Now I thought, They don't understand a thing!

"You don't know what friendship is! What if *I* said you shouldn't be best friends with Uncle Herbert and Aunt Marianne?" (I call the Löwbergs "Aunt" and "Uncle" because they and my parents have been friends for so long.)

"Don't be impertinent," said my father.

Mutti said, "Inge, try to understand—"

"I understand! You think the Vesselys are Nazis—"

My father put his hand over my mouth. "We said no such thing. Now, listen, this is important: Belonging to the Nazi Party is against the law in Austria. People get sent to jail for that, or into exile. We only say, don't see so much of Lieselotte. And we mean it, Inge. Is that clear?" He took his hand away.

"Clear as midnight!" I burst out. "She isn't Jewish, that's your reason! Well, Aunt Marianne isn't Jewish either, and you've not stopped being friends with her! It's not fair, it's not fair! It's as wrong as that Hitler is against people because they *are* Jewish!" I stomped out of the room and slammed the door.

They were going out that evening to the Café Schottentor, as usual. When they came into my room to kiss me good night, for the first time in my life I could not kiss them back.

As soon as they left, I sat down and wrote my heart out, how angry, disappointed, and betrayed I felt. I remember I began, "On this night I cease to be a child. Children do as their parents tell them. I won't, I can't, because they're wrong. I *will* stay best friends with Lieselotte."

I did. I kept on going there. If her mother was a Nazi, it didn't show in how she treated me. And Herr Vessely was hardly ever home. The few times he was there, it's true he didn't seem too thrilled to see me. Once he said to Lieselotte, right in front of me, "Don't you have any other friends?" He meant non-Jewish ones. I was so mortified, I pretended I hadn't heard. "Don't mind him," Lieselotte said later, "that's just the way he is."

She came to my house as much as ever. After all, my parents work all week and go away many weekends. And Mitzi didn't mind, and never told.

One thing changed: I couldn't invite her to birthday parties anymore. So I stopped having them. Instead my parents took me places: the year I was eleven, to a not too boring ballet about a fairy-doll. And last year, to the Spanish Riding School, to a performance by the Lippizaner horses, which Lieselotte would have loved. They are beautiful and can do dainty, complicated dance steps you'd never think horses would have the grace or coordination for.

Both those years we had another celebration, Lieselotte and I and Mitzi, that my parents didn't know about: Two years ago we went to a matinee of an American Shirley Temple film at the Urania Theater. And last year, to the Wurstelprater. People don't go there much in the wintertime. But most rides were open. We went on the Giant Ferris Wheel, of course, and on the scenic train through waterfalls, glaciers, and foreign lands; into the fun house; the spook house; and on the roller coaster (Mitzi didn't, she got scared). It was great.

The Vesselys moved away on Sunday, the seventh of Nov—

(Here's Evi again. But it's so hard for me to write about Lieselotte leaving that if I don't do it right this minute, I may never. So I said, "You can stay if you want to, Evi, but I have to finish what I'm doing, and don't ask me what, it's private." She said, "All right," and took a book, *Maya the Bee,* and is lying on my bed on her stomach, reading patiently.)

The seventh of November was a Sunday. Around nine in the morning I went over to their house. My parents were still sleeping.

Frau Vessely was packing last-minute stuff. Herr Vessely had left the week before. The moving men had come and taken away the furniture. "This place looks naked," Heinz said. It did, especially the lighter places on the floors where rugs had lain and the places on the walls where pictures had hung.

Frau Vessely wanted us to eat up what was left in the icebox, so we did, sitting on suitcases. We had some liverwurst, a sour pickle, a cold schnitzel, cold string beans, a little Liptauer cheese; and we drank up the last bit of milk.

"This is almost like an outing in the Wienerwald," said Frau Vessely. "See, there's even a fly!" One had flown in, and the sun streamed in now that the drapes were off. "So don't look like ten days' sow-weather, Lieselotte and Inge! Who knows, we might move back someday. Or maybe Inge can visit." But she knew and we knew she only said that to cheer us up.

Lieselotte gave me a present: a thick, green-bound book with a picture of a horse and rider on the cover. It was called *Beneath Distant Skies*.

"Turn to where the bookmark is," she said. "Read the part I marked."

I turned to there, and I read: "Then Trapper Charlie unsheathed his trusty hunting knife and pricked his finger with it; the noble Apache, Swift Eagle, unflinchingly did likewise; whereupon they mingled their blood in a cup of firewater, linked arms, raised the cup to their lips, and drank. Thus it came to pass that these two, though from worlds apart, became blood brothers. And blood brothers they remained unto their dying days."

"I let her have it to give to you," said Heinz.

"You mean you sold it to me," said Lieselotte. "I took the trash out for a whole week, remember?"

"You shouldn't have," I said. I was very moved.

"I wanted to," said Lieselotte.

We laughed at how formal we were being. Then we put our arms around each other and we cried.

"Sob sisters," said Heinz.

"I've seen *you* cry," said Lieselotte.

"My rear end, you have," said Heinz, only he used another word.

Frau Vessely was sitting on a suitcase, trying to get it shut. "Louse-boy, watch how you talk!" she yelled.

I had something for Lieselotte too: a silver pin of a skater in a twirly skirt I once won as second prize in a figure-skating contest.

Lieselotte pinned it to her dress.

"Now I have to go," I said.

Lieselotte said, "I'll walk you."

"No, there isn't time," said her mother. "Herr Hartmann will be here any minute." He was driving them to Munich.

We'd already hugged. I said *Tschüss*, fast, and I left.

When I got to the street, "Wait, Inge, catch!" Lieselotte called, leaning out the window.

I stuck the book under my arm and held both hands out. I concentrated for all I was worth on the thing she was throwing, as though it were our whole friendship. And I didn't miss, as I often do in games of catch.

It was wrapped in newspaper, like coins people throw down to street musicians.

I unwrapped it—her lucky pebble!

"Thanks! I'll keep it forever," I called, and ran home.

Mutti was in the kitchen, fixing a breakfast tray. It was Mitzi's Sunday off.

"Inge, is that you? Where were you?"

I went in to her. She saw the look on my face. "Did something happen?"

I decided to tell her. If she started scolding me for having stayed best friends with Lieselotte after all, if she said something like, Well, now you'll have to find someone else, I could always go into my room and shut the door.

She listened. She took a Memphis out of her housecoat pocket, lit it, and puffed. She let a big gust of smoke out and pulled me to her.

"Come have breakfast with Vati and me."

"I've already eaten."

"Keep us company then."

Vati was in pajamas, doing his Sunday-morning jumping jacks.

"Stop a minute, Franzl." Mutti told him where I'd been and that the Vesselys were moving away.

If either of them felt glad or relieved, they didn't show it.

"You know what I'd like to do? Go to Schönbrunn. We haven't been there in ages," said Vati.

Usually on Sundays they take their time over breakfast. For once they hurried, dressed, and we went.

We looked at all the animals. We bought elephant food and fed the real Schnurli Wurli, just like when I was small. We climbed up to the Glorietta and admired the view over the whole huge place with all the formal flower beds, fountains, pools, and palace buildings.

Then we had ham rolls, cake, and coffee with mountain peaks of whipped cream at the restaurant.

Even so, the day felt really long. I wondered if, from then on, all days would.

"*Heh,* look, it's snowing again," said Evi. She'd been so quiet, I forgot she was here. "Aren't you finished yet?"

"Almost."

I've gotten used to Lieselotte's being gone. But these last three months have felt longer than the six and a half years we were friends. And I haven't gotten used to the idea that we might not be friends anymore.

*Eleven p.m. Only one more hour left
of being 12, and of February 12!*

I just got back from supper with O.O. Was I ever stupid to think he's hard to talk to and not good company!

(Oh, by the way, I'm writing this with an elegant new Waterman fountain pen. It's sea-blue on the outside, and it holds enough ink for pages and pages, and it has a golden point, very fine! I threw out my old wooden pen holders and scratchy pen nibs. I'll never have to use them again!)

We went to the Chimneysweep, O.O.'s favorite restaurant. Red, blue, purple, pink, green, and yellow streamers dangled from the ceiling and from all the lamps because it's Fasching, carnival season, now. O.O. took down a purple and a pink one and draped them around my neck.

The owner of the Chimneysweep kissed my hand and said it was an honor to have me there. The chef came to our table. He's from the same place in Bohemia as O.O., and they've known each other for years.

While waiting for O.O. to fetch me, frankly, I'd been wondering what he and I were going to talk about. Before tonight our conversations went something like this: O.O.: Well, Inge, what are you learning at school these days? Me: Oh, nothing special. O.O.: Really not? Me: Uh-uh. And there we'd both be stuck.

Well, tonight—I wish I'd tried this sooner!—I'd decided to try something to get us unstuck, so before he asked the question, I greeted him with the answer, "Well, O.O., at school these days we're studying Cicero, isosceles triangles, the tributaries of the Danube, and English idioms, we're starting *Nathan the Wise* by Gotthold Ephraim Lessing, and we have to write a composition on the subject 'My Best Friend' for Monday."

It worked! His eyes, which often look droopy and remind me of a St. Bernard's, got all bright and happy-looking. He said, "*Nathan the Wise* is my favorite play! I've seen it fourteen times already at the Burgtheater. And, surprise, I am learning English idioms too. Listen—" and he gave me an example: "I am like a lion hungry, let us hurry therefore, quick."

On the way to the restaurant he said he always asks what I'm learning because he only had four years of formal schooling, so he's curious what he missed. He told me lots of things I never knew about his life: how poor and small his village in Bohemia was. That he would have had to become a tanner like his father because there were no other opportunities. But he couldn't stand the stink of animal hides drying in the sun. So when he was twelve, he "set out to seek his fortune," like young men in fairy tales, with his parents' blessings and a satchel on his back in which were the few things he owned. He came all the way on foot, except for a few rides he got in wagons (drawn by horses; there were no motorcars in those days).

When he got to Vienna, he rented, not even a room, just a

bed, in a strange family's apartment, in a building with one toilet for about thirty families. Some fun! And he got a job in a bank, adding up figures. Other people his age—girls too!—worked in factories, fourteen hours a day or more. He worked twelve hours a day, six days a week, and he earned less money to live on than I get for allowance.

Now he's a director of the Eldorado Life Insurance Company.

At the restaurant we talked about insurance, how it can't really insure your life, nothing can. It only insures your money, and maybe not even that so well in times like these.

O.O. says the times are very critical because Hitler is out to conquer the world, and the place he'll start with is Austria, it's only a question of how soon.

I said, "My father's sure he won't."

"I know. Your father is my very dear son-in-law, whom I love and respect, but when it comes to politics—"

"He's an optimist," I put in.

"Which is to say, he might as well have blinders on." O.O. crumbled up part of a roll. "Some weekend they picked for careening down mountains!"

O.O. doesn't know much about skiing. I said, "It's a good weekend, the snow is excellent. Lots of people picked this weekend for skiing, even Schuschnigg, I heard it on the radio."

"*Papperlapap,* don't believe it." O.O. leaned closer to me and said in a low voice, "Schuschnigg isn't skiing! He was called to Berchtesgaden, to Hitler's mountain palace, and at this very moment, while you and I are eating chicken soup with liver

dumplings, Schuschnigg's eating dirt out of Hitler's hand."
O.O. sounded worried and scornful at the same time.

"Really?" I tried to sound worried too. Actually I felt excited
and pleased to be taken into his confidence about such important matters.

Here's what O.O. thinks: Hitler is threatening that he will
send his soldiers and tanks and guns and so forth across our
borders (Germany has thousands more than we do) unless
Schuschnigg saves him the trouble.

"How do you mean?" I asked.

"Simple. By agreeing to Hitler's conditions: making the
Austrian Nazi Party legal; letting all our Nazis out of jail; inviting
back the ones who had to leave the country; allowing them to
hold their rallies, do their ugly propaganda stunts out in the
open." O.O. gave a bitter laugh. "That way they'll have the
country by the throat in no time, but from the inside, do you
understand what I mean? Hitler can sit back and watch it
happen, he won't have to budge." Suddenly O.O. stood up and
waved and called, "Hermann, Klara!"

A bald-headed man and a gray-haired lady came to our table.

"Klara, Hermann, what a surprise to see you! You must join
us," said O.O. "Let me present my granddaughter, Inge
Dornenwald. Inge, this is Herr and Frau Grossbart. Herr
Grossbart is my colleague at Eldorado, he has the office right
next to mine."

"It's a pleasure," they said, and sat down.

"It's a pleasure," I had to say too, though I'd much rather
they hadn't come.

They talked about who they think will become general director of Eldorado Life after Herr So-and-so retires and about Herr Grossbart's rheumatism and Frau Grossbart's sciatica and their adorable grandchild and dog, Putzi and Pucki, I didn't get it straight which was who. That was because I was still thinking about what O.O. and I had talked about before. I hoped O.O. was being too pessimistic. I thought, How awful if Hitler can push Schuschnigg around like that! I should be better informed, I decided, should read newspaper articles (though they are boringly written) instead of just the headlines. Then I'd know more when Susi König and Brigitte Wenzel have their arguments in school. Susi is a socialist. Brigitte is a Nazi. She doesn't say so, but she is, she thinks Hitler is wonderful.

One thing O.O. had said intrigued me: that the Nazis who left might be invited back. That wouldn't be good at all, I know. Yet I wished it. Because then the Vesselys—no. I decided it was better not to think about that.

On the streetcar home O.O. asked—I couldn't imagine why—whether the composition "My Best Friend" was supposed to be written in ink.

I answered, "Yes."

"Good!" He reached into his inside coat pocket and gave me my birthday present a little ahead of time—this pen!

Usually I avoid kissing him because of his mustache, which looks like a scrub brush. Now I did, right in front of the other streetcar passengers as we rattled down the Landstrasse-Hauptstrasse. I wasn't too embarrassed, and it didn't feel that scratchy.

Sunday, February 13!!!

As if the weather knew what day this is, it's sunny, the air is shining. I stuck my nose out the window when I first woke up, and I almost smelled spring!

Then I dived back under my eiderdown, and I hugged the feeling to me—I'd felt it all night long, during and between my dreams—that the something wonderful will happen. Yes! Today!

I must have dropped back off to sleep. Next thing I knew, there stood Mitzi with a silver tray of hot chocolate and a little *Guglhupf* with candles on it for my birthday breakfast. (*Guglhupf* is my second-favorite cake.)

Afterward I got dressed and said I was going for a walk.

"By yourself?" Mitzi doesn't think one should do things by oneself on one's birthday.

"But I want to!"

"Where will you go?"

"Oh, I'll just follow my nose." I meant I'd follow my something-wonderful feeling wherever it would lead me.

I walked to the Landstrasse-Hauptstrasse, past the market hall, and over into the Stadtpark. I squished along the soggy paths to the Weatherhouse, which has barometers, thermometers, and instruments that show from which direction the wind is blowing. Today it blew from the west. Good, Munich is west, I thought. But that was silly. One-fourth of all the places in the world are west of here.

Two little seven- or eight-year-old girls were playing

tag around the Weatherhouse. One bumped into me as she came tearing along. "Get out of my way!" she yelled.

"Listen, brat, I played tag here when you were still in your baby carriage," I said.

I went over to the lake. It's partly covered with slushy ice. I'd brought a stale salt stick along. I broke off pieces, threw them in. Fourteen ducks swam over, quacking hungrily, and fought for them.

When they finished eating, I continued on, past the Johann Strauss Memorial (where whoever was "it" in hide-and-seek used to stand and count to a hundred), down the flight of marble steps to the Wien embankment. The Wien is only a mud-colored trickle, not really a river. The embankment is a pleasant place, quiet, sheltered from the wind, and the walk is smoothly paved.

I happened to have a piece of chalk in my pocket. I stooped down, drew a line, just to test if the pavement was dry. And before I knew it, I'd drawn a whole set of Heaven and Hell boxes.

The pebble happened to be still in my pocket, from playing with Evi yesterday. Quickly I threw it into Box One, skipped to there, picked it up; into Box Two; and so on. I felt a little foolish playing all alone. But I'd already decided that if I got through all the boxes without missing, the wonderful something would all the more certainly happen.

I was up to Box Eight, usually a lucky one for me, when I heard footsteps down the stairs, looked around—and missed. An old man, an old lady, and a schnauzer came down the stairs. Interference, it doesn't count, I tried to think, but that was stupid. I quit, went home, and here I am, not discouraged. It's only one o'clock.

Later

Evi came down at three in the bulky blue sweater she has to wear skating. Her mother makes her go three times a week because it's "healthy." (Mine used to also, for the same reason, till I started *Gymnasium*. Now it's up to me when I go skating.)

"Here, Inge." Evi handed me a small white box tied with a silver string. I was really surprised. I've never given her a birthday present. I don't even know when her birthday is.

I opened the box. Inside, on a bed of white cotton, lay a silver Mogen Dovid on a thin silver necklace. "Oh, Evi, it's beautiful!"

"Aren't you going to put it on?"

I fastened it around my neck. When the star touched my skin, a jab of not-rightness went through me. That stupid scene about me and Hitler came into my head.

"Do you like it, Inge?"

"Oh, yes, thank you so much!"

Then Mitzi called us to the kitchen, and we finished up the *Guglhupf*.

Then Evi asked me, "Would you come skating with me?"

I was not one bit in the mood for the Vienna Ice Skating Rink. But I know what skating by yourself is like: at best, boring; at worst, boys trip you, and bunches of bigger girls pull your hat off and make fun of you for being alone. So I said, "All right." And we went.

The ice was good, and it wasn't too crowded. Evi is a better skater than you would guess from her short legs and dumpling shape. I taught her how to do the Swan. That's when you glide forward on one foot with your arms out like sails and one leg in the air behind you. She learned it pretty quickly.

Then we met Anni Hopf and Lisl Miller from my class and skated around with them a few times. Evi was so shy with them, she hardly opened her mouth. She thought it was an honor to skate with three *Gymnasium* girls.

Then Anni and Lisl left.

Then I saw him. He had on a dark blue beret, pulled over one ear. His light brown hair was cut shorter now, so his other ear seemed to stick out more. At first I was still too far away to see the color of his eyes, but I knew they'd be green, and they were. He stood behind the grillwork fence from where people on the street watch the skaters. He looked straight at me. "Heinz!" I yelled. But I couldn't slow down quick enough, I went gliding past. "Let go, Evi!" I yanked my hand out of her grasp, turned around, raced, wrong direction, back.

"Heinz, Heinz!" I shouted, waving both my arms at him.

He didn't wave back.

"*Heh*, it's me, Inge! Don't you know me anymore?"

He stared at me another moment, turned, and walked away.

"Heinz, Heinz, wait!"

Evi tugged at me. "Who's that?"

"Let go! Skate by yourself. I'll be back." I went tearing away.

"You're not allowed to skate in that direction," she shouted after me. "You'll get stopped!"

I skated like the wind, head down, bending forward, past everybody. A rink attendant skated over from the center. "The other way," he growled in thick Viennese and tried to turn me around. But I was already past him, almost at the exit, there it was.

I got off the ice and ran—if you can call it running—stumbling, clattering on my skates over the wooden plank floor, past the ticket booth, out, clunking along the sidewalk to the grill-work fence.

Only two women, a baby in a carriage, and an old man with a white beard were there. I looked up, down, and across the street. No Heinz in sight.

Clunking back to the rink entrance, I felt ridiculous and clumsy, aware of people wondering, What's that girl doing walking on her skates, ruining the blades?

At the ticket booth I showed my annual membership card. The lady shook her head. "It takes all kinds," she muttered, and let me back in.

Evi was waiting behind the booth. "Inge, who was that?"

"Just someone. Do me a favor, don't ask me anything." I headed for the locker room.

"We've only been here an hour! Don't you want to skate anymore?"

I went in. She followed. We changed to our shoes and left.

I walked fast. She had a hard time keeping up. "Inge, wait!"

I let her catch up. But I couldn't talk to her. I had to think my own thoughts. About mirages—people in the desert seeing palm trees, pools, a whole oasis in the distance, only when they get there, it's not real, it's just more sand. About doubles—people having other people who're not even related to them, whom they don't even know, who look exactly like them. But no one could look that much like Heinz! What was he doing in Vienna? Had he come by himself, just on a visit, or—or—I tried to stop myself there in case it wasn't so. But I couldn't think about anything else. And I kept seeing his blank green stare. . . .

At the corner stood a chestnut lady. Evi started to take out change to buy chestnuts.

"Don't. I won't wait for you." I rushed on.

When we got to our building, I said, "I'm sorry I acted so awful. I'll see you later."

"Aren't you going upstairs?"

"No, I have to go somewhere." To their old apartment building. I ran till I was out of breath, then walked, then ran again.

Lieselotte's old window was shut, no one looked out. Of course not, of course not, I jeered at myself, how would anyone know I'm on my way?

Just let Herr Magrutsch not come out his door, I hoped as I went into the entrance hall and smelled the familiar smell of turpentine and floor-scrubbing mixture. It's strange, entrance halls having their own distinct smells. Ours smells of permanent goulash. I made myself think about entrance-hall smells to get myself calm and make my heart stop pounding so fast.

I went up the stairs to the second, their old floor. I stood in front of their old apartment. My heart was knocking. I rang the bell.

Wau, wau, wau! came furious barking. A German shepherd, I can always tell. I ran—it's a reflex, I can't help it, whenever I hear one—back to the landing, down the stairs. By the time someone opened the door, I was already down on the first floor.

"You wait, next time I'll catch you," a man's voice shouted. He thought it was children playing the old game Ring a Doorbell and Run.

Could that have been Herr Vessely? After all, I don't know his voice that well. No, I decided, it couldn't. They wouldn't have gotten a dog like that, not the one kind I hate. Lieselotte wouldn't have let them. Besides, I thought, starting for home, how could they have gotten their old apartment back so easily? It's hard to find apartments these days, and some other family had probably already moved in. So maybe they didn't have an apartment yet, were looking for one, were staying in a hotel meantime. And then I thought, Hotels have telephones!

"Mitzi, did I get any telephone calls?" I shouted breathlessly, opening the door, throwing my coat off.

"Why, no, gracious Fräulein." She mock-curtsied and laughed. "The Count of Hohenlohen and the Baroness von Frangipangi haven't called up yet to inquire after your health today," meaning, since when do I get telephone calls? It's true, I hardly ever do. Of the girls in my class with whom I'm friendly, the only ones who even have telephones are Susi König and Anni Hopf, and they call each other up a lot more often than either one calls me.

"And since when do you drop your things like a snake her skin?" Mitzi hung my coat up. "What's wrong with you, anyway? You look awful! Where have you been? I heard Evi on the stairs, she came home over half an hour ago. I thought you were together!" She put her hand on the back of my neck and pushed me into the kitchen. "If you're going to wait till all hours to have dinner when your parents come home, you'd better get something nourishing into you now or you'll collapse."

I swallowed down a few spoonfuls of some soup she'd made. And I poured out to Mitzi that I'd seen Heinz and how he'd acted and that I'd gone to their old house. "They're not there, but, Mitzi, I think they're back in Vienna, I just have a feeling they are!"

"Go on! You fell on the ice and you scrambled your brains, that's how you sound. That couldn't have been Heinz, or he'd have greeted you. And if they were coming back, Lieselotte would have let you know."

"Maybe she couldn't! What if it happened so all of a sudden she didn't have time?"

"What if no word 'if' were there? My father'd be a millionaire." Mitzi loves that saying, and she doesn't even have a father! "Finish that soup. Then you can help me peel these mushrooms. Want to?"

"No, I can't!" I suddenly thought, The composition's due tomorrow, and I haven't even started! It loomed before me like a very steep mountain I had to climb.

I went into my room.

"Go lie down, you got overtired," Mitzi called.

I took my school composition notebook and my fountain pen and went into the study. That's where the telephone is.

I sat down at my father's desk. I turned to a fresh page in the composition notebook. I wrote "February 13, 1938" in the right-hand corner, and on the next line, in the center, "My Best Friend."

I looked up at the telephone, and I thought, Damn you, telephone, ring!

It stared at me like a spiteful monster bird with a round wide-open black beak through which came no sound, no sound.

Then my mind went blank. As blank as the page before me, as the silence around me, as the big empty desert must be. I felt like I was in a desert too—hot, and my lips and throat were dry. And I thought, Lieselotte's different now, she doesn't care about me anymore, she doesn't want to know me.

I stood up. It seemed as if those thoughts had made me ache all over. I went to get a drink of water and this book, and wrote all this in here.

Later, on the rottenest day of my life

It's selfish to call this the rottenest day of *my* life when my mother is having awful pain and can't even stand. It's the rottenest day of *her* life.

At a quarter past eight the telephone finally rang.

All my hope came rushing back. I grabbed the receiver. "Hello?"

"Ingelein—" My father! All my hope flew out the window, even though the window was shut.

How come you answered so fast? I thought he'd ask. He doesn't like my being in the study at his desk. He didn't ask. For a second there was only crackling and static.

"How was the snow? Did you have a good time? Are you calling from the railroad station?"

"Yes. The snow was fine. Inge, listen, there's been a little accident—"

Crackle, crack, went the wires. Neck and Leg Break, I almost heard them say.

"Your mother—"

Broke her neck, it roared into my ear, it thundered in my head. "What happened to her?"

"Be calm, Ingelein. Nothing so terrible. She hurt her leg."

"Did she break it?"

"We don't know yet. Uncle Herbert says it might be just a sprain." (Uncle Herbert is a doctor.) "We're lucky he's with us. I just wanted to prepare you so it won't be such a shock."

"Let me talk to her!"

"Not now, when we come home. We should be home in forty minutes. Meantime, I'm sorry about spoiling your birthday."

"Don't even think about that!"

I feel too awful to write about how it was when they came home.

Monday, February 14

I have the grippe. Dr. Hecht was just here. So much has happened, yesterday seems like an age ago. I'll start where I left off:

My father carried her in. Uncle Herbert and Aunt Marianne and Tommi carried their own, plus my parents' packs and skis and poles.

My mother's face was blotting-paper gray. Her eyes looked

sunken in. But she forced herself to smile. "Unfortunately, Inge, you have a very clumsy skier for a mother."

I kissed her. Her cheeks felt cold and tasted sweaty. "Which leg is it? Does it hurt a lot?"

"Happy birthday, darling—oh!" She tried very hard not to, but she groaned, and her face twisted.

"Let's get you to bed," Vati said. He and Mitzi carried her into the bedroom.

I followed. "Mutti, can I do anything for you?"

"Yes, get out of here. Franzl, you too. Thank the Löwbergs for me. Enjoy the dinner. Mitzi will make me comfortable."

Uncle Herbert is a general practitioner. He called up an X-ray doctor he knows and made an appointment for Mutti for today.

Aunt Marianne said she'd take her there.

Tommi said, "I hope it's nothing serious." He turned to me. "Your mother's really not a clumsy skier."

I said, "I know."

"Herbert, Marianne, you too, Tommi, I don't know what we'd have done without you," said my father, and started to thank them.

"What are friends for?" said Aunt Marianne.

Then they left.

Vati and I sat down to dinner. Mitzi had put a lace tablecloth on, and the good silver, and the good Rosenthal gold-rimmed dishes. She'd taken the third place setting away. The table looked big and empty.

The main course was roast venison. You can only buy that when it is in season. It's supposed to be the best-tasting meat there is. And mushroom gravy, roast potatoes, and cucumber salad with dill.

"Mitzi outdid herself," said my father.

"Mm." I took one bite of everything.

He told me how the accident happened. My mother was going down a very steep slope in *Schuss*. A ski instructor they had made friends with had given her some pointers on how to improve her technique. She was showing off a little, my father guessed. Anyway, she went too fast. Her skis hit a rock hidden under the snow. He said three times I shouldn't worry, she would be all right.

In between bringing out dishes Mitzi kept going into the bedroom to Mutti.

I cleared the table. That way Mitzi didn't see all the food we left over.

Then she said Mutti wanted us.

Mutti sat in bed propped up against pillows. She had an even brighter smile on.

On my father's night table stood another birthday cake, hazelnut, my favorite kind. (Mitzi had baked it and hidden it away while I was out this morning.)

Mutti's night table was turned into my birthday table, heaped with presents. She said, "I wouldn't have missed this for anything."

That meant, if it were not my birthday, she would have gone straight from the station to the hospital, and her leg would already be in a cast or something instead of hurting her so much.

The presents were all things I'd wanted: a brown leather

pocketbook I'd admired in a store window on the Kärntner-strasse; a blue pullover; a crystal inkwell from which to fill my new pen; a leather-bound book of poems by Heine; and one present I never dreamed I'd get before I was at least fourteen—a ticket to the opera, the Vienna State Opera! That is so famous, people come here from all over the world just to go to it. My parents go quite often too, and I envy them every time. Whenever I pass by the building (it's very majestic, with many arches and decorative statues in niches), I always imagine what it will be like when I finally go in there to a performance.

The ticket is for March 8, to *Lohengrin*. That's my mother's favorite opera. I held it in my hand, not saying anything. My parents thought I was speechless with surprise. Yes, but the surprise was, I wasn't glad, I didn't want to go!

"I'll take you," said Vati. "Unless of course by then you already have another admirer." Now he smiled forcedly.

"Unless of course, I'm fine again, then *I'll* go," said my mother, oh, so cheerfully. Her cigarette smoldered in the ashtray. Instead of taking puffs she clutched and unclutched her hands, that's how badly her leg hurt.

I sat on the edge of her bed. She clutched my hand and stroked it.

Every other year, after getting my presents, I've always said, "This is the best birthday I've ever had." I knew she was waiting for me to say that. The room was so quiet, you could hear the sheets rustle as she shifted around.

"An angel must be floating by," said Mitzi. "Your guardian angel, Inge."

71

No, it's my devil, I wanted to say, I felt so bad, so bad! I thought, This is the worst birthday of my life!

"Thank you a lot for all my presents," I managed to say. My lips felt crackly, my mouth felt parched. The rest of me felt burning up, and my head throbbed, *Bumm, bumm, bumm.* "You must always tell us when you are not feeling well," my mother has drummed into me ever since I can remember. I did not tell them. They had enough to worry about. I kissed them good night, quick on top of their heads so they wouldn't notice how hot my face was. I took my presents, went to my room, started to write in here, felt too awful, went to bed.

This morning when I woke up, they were gone. Mitzi said my mother's leg hurt so much, my father called a taxi at a quarter to six and took her to the hospital where Uncle Herbert works.

"You look sick yourself." Mitzi took my temperature. I had a fever. She called up Dr. Hecht.

I went to lie on Mutti's bed, like when I was little.

Mitzi brought me chamomile tea. She thinks that cures everything. I didn't feel like reading or writing. She turned on the radio. A symphony came on, I was already asleep when they said by whom.

Next thing I heard, still half asleep, was a voice saying, ". . . not on a ski holiday, as was believed . . ." Oh, good, I thought with huge relief, there wasn't any accident, I only dreamed it! But it was the news announcer, and he was talking about Schuschnigg, not about my parents. Schuschnigg had been holding "talks" with Hitler, just like O.O. had said!

"Details have not yet been made available," said the news announcer.

Mitzi came in, turned the radio off. "Your father called while you were sleeping. He says your mother's better."

"Is her leg broken?"

"No."

Then Fredl came by. "You're just in time, she's burning up," said Mitzi for a joke. Fredl pretended to turn a firehose on me and made a noise like rushing water to amuse me, so I laughed.

Mitzi turned the radio back on. "Talks between our countries' two chancellors were highly satisfactory," said the news announcer.

"Sure," said Fredl, "so's crawling naked through mud." Only *mud* was not the word he used.

Mitzi laughed. "Shut your muddy mouth!"

"You wait, you'll see swastikas blooming in people's lapels by spring." Either Fredl said that, or I imagined it out of my fever.

Mitzi teased, "What makes you such a know-it-all?"

"I may not know it all, but I know what's soft and round," he said, and pinched her behind. She giggled.

I slept some more, drank more chamomile tea, my fever went down, the day dragged on.

Finally Vati came home. He told me Mutti has a pleasant room, the nurses are nice to her, Uncle Herbert stopped in to see her, "and she's much more comfortable than yesterday." With all this good news, though, he didn't smile. He was tired, I guessed.

"Will I be able to visit her?"

"No, Ingelein. Unfortunately they don't allow visitors who are under fourteen."

Tuesday, February 15

I'm not sick anymore. But Dr. Hecht said I still have to stay in bed today. I'm bored, I'm in a bad mood, there's nothing I feel like doing. . . .

Later

The telephone rang.

I asked, "Who was it, Mitzi?"

"N-nobody."

"Come on, who?"

"How would you like a nice slice of rye bread and goose fat?"

"Don't try to distract me. Tell me who called."

She shook her head.

"Then I'll tell my father Fredl was here again, and where he pinched you, and so forth."

"All right. Your father called. Your mother didn't break her leg, she broke her whole hip. The left one. They have to open it up and try to nail it back together. With two nails made of steel. A big one and a small one. It's a new operation. Only one surgeon in all Vienna knows how to do it. His name is Dr. Feuerwerker. And he's doing it. Right now. You father will call again when it's over. He said not to tell you—"

She collapsed on the bed and sobbed. I patted her hair. She recently got a permanent wave. Her hair felt frizzy.

She sat up and wiped her eyes. "*You're* the one who should be crying."

"I know." I wanted to. But it was like when someone is in the toilet with you waiting for you to pee, and so you can't, even though you have to.

Mitzi took her rosary out of her apron pocket and touched the beads, saying Ave Marias under her breath.

Then she said, "I have to get my work done. Will you be all right?"

"Yes."

How long does that operation take? I am trying not to blink. Whenever I do, I see my mother with her eyes shut, lights glaring down on her, doctors standing over her, like ghosts, in doctor gowns, holding instruments. Mutti, Mutti, be all right! I'd write those words a thousand times if I thought that would help.

I think I'll write her portrait:

HANNAH REICHMANN DORNENWALD

She's never sick. She never catches colds or the grippe. She doesn't even get headaches. She is very energetic and likes getting things done. She must hate lying still, she must have hated the ether, being made not to feel. I can't, I don't want to, imagine what that's like.

She is thirty-six years old and still beautiful. She has very dark brown, almost black, eyes. They slant down at the corners. Her eyelashes are thick and short. She says they used to be really long, but they got singed from lighting cigarettes. She has a dainty nose and smooth, fair skin with hardly any wrinkles yet. She is not much taller than me and has a lovely figure, slender, not skinny like mine. Her hair is dark, dark brown and turning gray in front. She is letting it. I'm glad. I don't like dyed hair. She also does not pluck her eyebrows into thin, thin arches like ladies do who want to look like fashion models in magazines.

When I was small, I used to stand on a chair in the bathroom and watch her get ready for going out in the evening. I was fascinated by how she made "water waves" in her hair and how neatly she put rouge and a little lipstick on. Best of all I loved how when she was done, she would smile into the mirror. I told myself that seeing two of her looking so beautiful and perfect made up for later, when I would wish I could see her, but she would be out.

She is a perfectionist. She thinks you should either do things very well or not do them at all. She managed to hide that when she was watching me after my first ski lessons, and kept encouraging me even though I fell down twenty times and got my skis crossed and was as clumsy as if I had two left legs.

When she was young, she used to play the violin. One day she heard her favorite violinist play at a concert and got so impatient with how *she* sounded by comparison, she gave her violin away. She says that was childish of her. But she's just as glad. She says she has enough to do, working for Huber Verlag and being my mother.

When she was my age, there were only two *Gymnasiums* for girls in all of Vienna. She went to one of them. You had to be extra intelligent to get accepted. She does not brag about this. But it's so.

My mother was fourteen when Grandmother Ida died. Grandmother Ida had wanted to be a physicist or something like that herself. But in her time that was almost impossible for a woman. She would have been proud that my mother went to university and studied literature and is an editor of books for Huber Verlag. That is quite an unusual job for a woman. My mother is proud of it, and it means a lot to her.

I think she had a lot of admirers in her youth, before she met my father. She once showed me some old dance programs she saved, and the blanks were all filled in with names of young men who'd reserved special dances with her.

She and my father met on a mountain top. Here is how I have always imagined it: them climbing up from different sides; catching sight of each other; falling into each other's arms; and coming down together with their arms around each other all the way.

They have been married for fifteen years.

When I was born, she took half a year's leave of absence from Huber Verlag. Then she went back to work.

When I was little, I used to wish we didn't have a maid and that she'd stay home with me and do things like clean and go marketing and cook and bake.

Now I only wish she were all right again. And that I'd said Neck and Leg Break. And that the operation were over and I could see her. . . .

Mitzi came in and sat with me. Finally, finally Vati called. The operation was successful! Vati said the surgeon said that in a month or so she'll hop around as nimbly as the Easter hare, and her hip will be as good as new.

Later

I can go to school tomorrow. I'd better write my composition now.

Still later

Well, I opened my composition notebook to the page dated Sunday, entitled "My Best Friend." I faced what Sunday brought and what it did not bring.

It did not bring me Lieselotte back. If she ever does return, she'll be different. She'll probably act just like Heinz.

After facing all that, I felt very emptied out, but calm and self-controlled. I tore that page out. I wrote today's date, and the title again, and then the composition—about Upstairs-Evi Fried. Her appearance. (I didn't write that she's dumpling shaped. I just wrote that she's plump.) How long I've known her. That she had diphtheria and an operation when she was little. That both she and her parents are always very nice to me. How lucky it is to have a friend who lives right in the same building, whom I can see whenever I want. And so forth.

It came to three and a quarter pages, orderly and ordinary.

And now, before I go to bed, I'll put this book away in my PRIVATE, DO NOT TOUCH box.

Two

Dear Book O.O. gave me for Chanukah, nearly three weeks have passed since I last wrote in your pages . . . No, that's dumb. This book is not alive, and I won't pretend it is. I've missed it, though.

The reason I'm writing in here again is something O.O. said this morning.

I met him down on the Franz Joseph Quai after school, to go to temple. It was windy on the quai. His hat blew off and into a flower bed. I picked it up and saw a yellow crocus pushing through the ground. "Look, O.O.," I said, "it's spring!"

"Indeed," he answered in his funny English, "a season of storms, no? Be so kind and correct if I have maked mistake."

Made, the past tense of the irregular verb *to make* is *made,* Mr. Cookson, our English teacher at school, would insist. I let it go. "No mistakes."

"Thank you nicely." O.O. felt encouraged and went on, "Spring is a pleasant season to emigrate, no? I hope also you will. I sound to you foolish?"

"Not foolish." The word *emigrate* makes me shiver, though.

O.O. already did it once in his life. Now he's almost all ready to do it again.

He applied a year ago for his American quota number. (He already thought then that things would go badly for Austria.) Now his quota number has come up, and America will let him in. He has his passport, exit permit, transit visa to Italy (he'll take a boat from Genoa). And when he gets to America, he'll even have a job there because the Eldorado Life Insurance Company has its main office in New York.

He moved out of his apartment last week. His furniture is stored in a warehouse. It will be shipped to him when he finds a place to live in New York.

Right now he is staying with us, in the study, waiting for two things to happen:

One is, he wants to see my mother on her feet, able to walk again, at least a little.

The other thing is, he wants to be sure my father applies for our American quota numbers.

Vati doesn't want to. He doesn't see why he should give up his business, our comfortable apartment, our whole way of life. He thinks things may well turn out all right for Austria, that Schuschnigg is doing his best to keep Austria independent. And if worse does come to worst and we have to emigrate, Vati would rather go somewhere nearby—Switzerland or Czechoslovakia, for instance, where things are not so different, where he'd have a better chance to earn a living than in the "New World." He thinks he wouldn't fit in there.

"Don't fool yourself," O.O. says, "those countries will close their borders once people start fleeing. Besides, those countries won't be safe themselves for long."

He and Vati argue about this a lot. Mutti agrees more and more with O.O. I don't know whose side I'm on. Of course I want Vati to be right. It's scary to imagine packing up and leaving, moving somewhere new and strange. But it's also exciting, and sometimes I wish we would.

Anyway, this morning I only went to temple because he'd asked me to. It wasn't my turn in the system.

I have to explain about that: There are nine Jewish girls in our class at school. We are required to go to temple every Saturday and must hand in attendance slips to prove that we were there. But we have an old, tried and true system whereby each week only three of us go. Instead of taking seats right away we slip inconspicuously out again by the side door, and in again, out again, in again. That way we collect enough attendance slips for everyone. Sometimes I think the ushers who hand out the slips are not so blind and are playing along with us and probably had a system just like ours when they were in *Gymnasium*. In any case, it works.

I told O.O. about it. He laughed. He said, "Oh, well, it just goes to show, there are many ways of being Jewish."

"How do you mean?"

"Well, of course, in the first place it's Jewish to want to go to temple. But it's also Jewish not to want to if it isn't of your own free will. So it's not so very un-Jewish to make up a system against being forced. Don't you think?"

I was glad he saw it like that.

Temple is different, it's better, when you go with somebody who really wants to. Or else it was because the rabbi, Dr. Taglicht, talked about something interesting: Cain and Abel. He said that quibbling about whether or not those two actually lived, and if so, where and when, is missing the point of the story.

The point is, brother murdered brother. And though the world has come a long way since then, brother murder is still going on, more than ever.

Then he spoke about Jews in Germany: Some are losing their means of earning a living; some, their homes; and students, their places in schools. He said we in Austria must face with open eyes that the same, maybe worse, may lie ahead for us. Yet we must also keep our faith in humanity and God. And if that's a paradox, well, it's not the first in the history of Jews.

O.O. knows Dr. Taglicht. Afterward he went up to him and introduced me. Dr. Taglicht shook hands with me. I may come again next Saturday, even though it still won't be my turn.

Walking home, I put my hands in my pockets and felt the "lucky" pebble, still in there. It gave me a pang, but not so very sharp. Compared to Cain and Abel, losing a friend—even one like Lieselotte—seems a lesser tragedy.

"O.O., look," I whispered. A man with a red, white, and black swastika badge in his lapel came toward us. I waited till he passed, then I asked, "Aren't those badges forbidden anymore?"

"Officially, yes. But the police are closing their eyes. Also to that sort of thing." O.O. pointed to a wall.

I looked. JEWS, GO CROAK! was scrawled there in red letters almost a meter high. I looked away, fast. Then I wanted to look again, but I didn't. I kept my eyes to the ground, as though the wall scrawl would sting them, burn them.

I've seen scrawls like that before, and I'm always torn between wanting to look and wanting not to. I told this to O.O.

"Hm," he said, thinking about it. "Do you want my advice?"

"Yes."

"You should look—as hard as you need to, to know what you are seeing. Then you should write down what you saw."

"Why?" I suddenly felt embarrassed. I thought of my first try at writing, that Devil story with all the commas in it. Did Mutti tell him about that? I felt my ears turn red.

O.O. thought they were that color just from the cold. He took his gray silk scarf off. He put it over my head and tied it under my chin. "There." He put his coat collar up against the wind. "It's good to write down what you see, also, how you feel about it. It helps you understand things better. And later it helps you remember."

"I do write things down, sometimes. At least I did. In that book you gave me."

He clasped his hands behind his back and started walking faster. He asked, "Are there still blank pages in it?"

"Yes."

"So write on them."

Just then a red and white steamboat chugged past on the blue-greenish whitecapped Danube Canal, heading west, puffing white smoke into the blue air. A flock of gulls followed it, shrieking and swooping, making lovely loops and arches in the air. I mention this because it was part of the moment. And because I don't expect to write down only the awful things in here, such as how many Nazi badges and anti-Semitic scrawls on walls I see.

———

Later

One important thing to write down here is, Mutti came home last Monday from the hospital. Some feelings go without saying, so I'm not going to try to put into words how I felt to see her again.

Vati rented her a hospital bed. The head part can be raised and lowered, and it has different weights attached by ropes and pulleys. She has to exercise with those. It's too big to fit into their bedroom, so it's in the living room, which has now also become a combination hospital (when the doctor visits and when she exercises), office (when she does her work for Huber Verlag—a freckle-faced messenger boy named Gustl brings her manuscripts to work on every week), coffeehouse (when friends come), and bedroom (when she sleeps).

Dr. Feuerwerker came to see her Tuesday. He ordered a pair of crutches, for later. He says her hip is mending well but slowly. She has to give it time. He told her not to try walking for another two weeks.

Oh, and the living room is also like an indoor garden because so many people who visit bring flowers. We're running out of vases.

Now it's eleven at night, and company is here: the Löwbergs, the Plattaus, and Frau Kronisch. It's a farewell evening for Frau Kronisch. Her husband is on a lecture tour in America in a city called Tschicago. They invited him to stay there, so she and their children can join him right away, they don't have to wait for their quota numbers to come up. She is very happy about it.

Frau Plattau says, "I envy you."

Now they are discussing the Nazi rally in Graz last week. Vati says it was brave of Schuschnigg to send soldiers and put a stop to it. Yes, says Herr Plattau (he's my father's business partner), but tomorrow there will be an even bigger rally in Linz, and Schuschnigg won't be able to stop it on account of Seyss-Inquart.

Seyss-Inquart (I happen to know from reading the paper) is the new Minister of Security. And he's a Nazi, he wants the rally. So he'll tell the police to help it along, and they will.

By the way, his name sounds like a certain dirty word, so naturally there are lots of jokes and poems going around about him. Uncle Herbert is starting to tell one.

"Don't be childish," Herr Plattau interrupts. "Seyss-Inquart is no laughing matter. He's personally delivering our country into Hitler's hands."

"Maxl, where's your sense of humor?" says Vati.

"I left it in the long, long line outside the American consulate," says Herr Plattau.

"You hear that, Franz? And you, you stubborn mule, still haven't applied," says my mother.

"Because I heard a funny rumor: Not all the streets in America are paved with gold. Besides, who says we're done for?" Vati offers everybody cognac.

They discuss whether Italy, England, and France would really come to Austria's rescue as they promised in treaties.

Uncle Herbert tells a Goering joke.

"In Germany people are put to death for jokes like that," Herr Plattau says.

"You really are a spoilsport," says Uncle Herbert.

Talk, talk, my hand hurts from trying to keep up with it. I've heard enough. This is one of the times I wish something would happen. If worse is coming, let it come already!

Sunday morning, March 6

No, I take it back, I didn't mean it! *Teu, teu, teu* and knock on wood! Let nothing happen to spoil April Fools'!

At two in the morning Mitzi came into my room. She switched on my bed lamp. I was in the middle of a dream about Mutti walking without crutches, like before. I pulled my eiderdown up to my nose and tried to stay asleep.

"Sloth, wake up!" Mitzi yanked the eiderdown down. "Want to see something?" She held her left hand out to me. On her ring finger was a golden ring. She moved her hand so the stone— about the size of a fly's eye—caught the light. "What do you say to that? That's not a piece of glass in there! That's a real diamond, and the gold is fourteen karats."

I blinked, I rubbed my eyes. "It's beautiful! Are you getting married?"

"Whatever gives you that idea?" Her eyes sparkled brighter than the diamond.

"To Fredl?"

"No, to the Emperor of China!"

"When?"

"On April Fools'! Fredl always said only fools get married, so when better?"

"That's wonderful, Mitzi, congratulations! But what are *we* going to do?"

"Oh, you'll find someone else."

"No, we won't, not like you."

"Oh, sure, there's hundreds of girls fresh from the country, needing jobs. Inge, listen . . ."

"What?"

"Want to be my bridesmaid?"

"Me? You mean it?"

"No. I only asked because I don't mean it."

"Oh, Mitzi, I'd love to!"

"Shh, you'll wake your mother."

I was sitting up in bed. She put her cheek against mine. "All right, then that's set." She pushed me back down. "Now go back to sleep."

Oh, it will be so thrilling! I'll have a beautiful dress, Mitzi will sew it, she'll let me pick out the material. And hers is a family heirloom, with a long, long train, which I will carry for her all the way down the aisle. And afterward I'll stand outside on the church steps with everybody, throwing rice . . . oh, I can't wait!

It will be a medium-sized wedding. Most of the people will be from Fredl's side: his parents, four brothers, two sisters, three grandparents, and I don't know how many uncles and aunts; also, most of his fire brigade, plus their wives or the girls they are engaged to.

From Mitzi's side there will only be her great-grandmother, who brought her up, if she is strong enough to make the trip from Mondsee; her older sister, Alma, and Alma's husband,

Johann, from Mondsee too; three of Mitzi's friends from the neighborhood; and my parents, they are invited too, of course; and me.

It will be held in the Kolodnitz Church, right behind my old school, in the morning. (I'll have to take the day off from school!) Afterward there will be a wedding breakfast at Fredl's parents' apartment with champagne and wedding cake, to which of course I'm also invited.

Twenty-six more days. Oh, please, oh, please, let nothing prevent it!

Later

Mutti got into an awful mood about it. Of course not in front of Mitzi. She congratulated her "heartily." But as soon as Mitzi was out of earshot, she said, "That's all I need! Flat on my back and having to train a new girl fresh from the country!"

"It's a month away, you'll be hopping around by then," Vati said. But he was in a bad mood too.

We had the radio on. All of a sudden it started playing the national anthem—ours, I thought. The melody is the same. Then I noticed the words, *"Deutschland, Deutschland über Alles/Über Alles in der Welt . . ."* And I asked, "How come they're playing the German national anthem?"

"It's like with the swastikas in people's lapels," said O.O. "It's allowed now."

"Inge, the weather's brightening up, you should be outdoors," said my father.

"You should let her listen, Franz," said O.O.

"Oskar, if you don't mind, *I'll* decide what's best for my daughter."

"Inge, don't you want to go skating?" said Mutti. "The season's nearly over, you should go while you can." Meantime she was raising, then lowering her leg, trying to pull up one of the weights. "Ask Evi if she wants to."

"Evi always wants to. *I* don't." I watched her lower her leg another two centimeters. Sweat ran down her forehead. Her put-on smile turned into a grimace.

"All right, I'll go."

When I got upstairs, the Frieds' radio was blaring.

"This is Radio Linz, Upper Austria. We here are celebrating German Day, we are marching, a hundred thousand strong, bla bla," and I could hear shouting, *"Sieg Heil, Sieg Heil,"* in the background. Then somebody started a speech: "Folk comrades and comradesses—"

"Who is that? Seyss-Inquart?" I asked.

Herr Fried scowled. He's even worse than my father; he thinks "children" shouldn't have any idea what's going on. "Go, go already. Don't pay attention, you're better off skating," he said.

"But slowly, skate slowly, don't hurt yourselves," said Frau Fried.

Evi is even more ignorant than I was at her age. She doesn't know anything about anything. On the way to the skating rink we passed a cleaner's store with JEW PIG scrawled on the window.

Evi thought the cleaner must have done something really bad to whoever had scrawled those words.

"Oh, Evi, don't be so dense! The cleaner didn't do anything. It's just anti-Semitism," I tried to explain.

"Let's not talk about it," Evi said.

Monday, March 7

This morning, going to school, for the first time I saw Nazis in action. I hid behind a kiosk. At first I was too scared to watch. But I made myself, and the more I saw, the madder I got. It was all over some bunting. Last week Schuschnigg gave a speech asking everyone to be patriotic and stand behind the Fatherland Front, which is standing behind Austria. So then people put out lots of flags and draped red-white-red bunting from building to building all around the Ringstrasse. Well, when I got to the corner of Ringstrasse and Karl Lueger Platz, where I usually cross, some men were trying to rip the bunting down. At first it looked like a circus act, with thinner men standing on the shoulders of fatter ones to reach the bunting because it was so high up. When I came nearer, I saw that all those men had swastika armbands on. Next thing an open truck roared up and a bunch of men jumped out. These had red-white-red armbands on; they were from the Fatherland Front. They tried to pull the top Nazis off the bottom ones. One landed with a loud thud on the pavement. It sounded as though his head was smashed. But then he got to his feet and punched the man who'd pulled him down, and *he* fell with a thud. There was lots more of this. Then the police arrived. I thought, Good. That's because I'm used to thinking of the police as helping people who are in the right. They wore helmets and had truncheons. Well, they arrested the Fatherland Front men! For a crazy moment I wanted to shout, *Heh,* you can't do that! Of course I didn't. I stayed behind the kiosk and watched them shove the Fatherland Front men into the police wagon while the Nazis got away.

When the police wagon was gone, the Nazis came back, joking, clapping one another on the back, and they ripped down more bunting. Nobody stopped them. Some passersby shook their heads. Some didn't even do that!

A block away from school I met Susi König and Gerda Weidenau. They were in a furious argument. Susi had seen a fight near the Burgring, just like the one I saw, and the police had arrested the patriotic Austrians there too. "You must be crazy," Gerda said. "The police wouldn't do that."

Then just the person we didn't need, Herta Kröger, came along and mixed into it. "The Fatherland Front men are the hoodlums," she said, and told us that she'd seen ten of them start a fight, for no reason, with only four, well, maybe six men who just happened to be wearing swastika armbands, but that didn't mean anything, they were just minding their own business, feeding the pigeons in the Volksgarten.

"You liar," Susi said.

"No, you're the liar," Herta said. "Isn't she a liar, Gerda?"

Gerda said "Yes" and got behind Herta.

I moved closer to Susi to show I was backing her.

Herta hauled out. Her fist was two centimeters from Susi's chin.

"Look out!" Gerda said, and Herta put her arm down. Frau Direktor Waldemar was coming. She wears thick glasses. Even with them on she is very nearsighted.

"Good morning, Frau Direktor," we all said after quickly readjusting our faces.

"Good morning, girls."

If she had caught us fighting, she would have given us detentions, which would have been very inconvenient for me because Mitzi was picking me up after school to go to Gerngross.

Gerngross is the biggest department store in Vienna. We looked through bolts and bolts of all sorts of material and finally picked the loveliest: shimmery, rustling blue taffeta for my bridesmaid's dress. We also bought blue velvet ribbon for the sash, and hooks and snaps and trimming. My parents are paying for it, of course. It will be long and flowing and will have a waistline instead of just hanging, the way most of my dresses do.

Too bad some elves can't come and finish it overnight! Because tomorrow is the opera, and I wish I could wear it. Oh, well, I'll have to wear my old "good" brown velvet with its sweet little white piqué collar, in which I look about eleven and a half years old at the most.

Aside from how I'll look, I got over not being glad about going. That was just part of how I felt about Mutti's accident, plus feeling sick myself, on my birthday when they gave me the ticket. I've been looking forward to it a lot. In fact, I've been counting the hours till tomorrow night. I've read the libretto too. Unlike a lot of other opera stories, *Lohengrin* is not hard to follow or boring; on the contrary, I can't wait to see how they'll work it that a boy gets bewitched into a swan and back right on stage, before the audience's eyes.

At this very moment I hear Mutti through the wall, humming the aria in which Elsa (sister of the swanboy) sings about a shining knight she saw in her dream.

I wish Mutti could go with us. I asked her if she minds a lot, missing it.

"Oh, no, I've seen it so many times," she said. But she minds. A new tenor who is supposed to be very good is making his debut. "You'll have a wonderful time, Inge. It will be the most exciting evening in your life!"

Wednesday, March 9

It was, it was! But not the way my mother thought . . .

And now I am a "baked fish." (Dumb expression, but they use it for young girls who newly feel the way I do.) And I still haven't washed my left hand. . . .

The Opera House is where the Kärntnerstrasse meets the Opernring. The Kärntnerstrasse is Vienna's most elegant street, especially in the evening, with taxis and private motorcars driving by and people getting out, dressed for going to the opera and to expensive restaurants.

Well, yesterday (it was pleasant weather, so we walked) there were no taxis, no cars, no traffic at all on the Kärntnerstrasse.

The whole broad street was full of people, forty, fifty, or more abreast, hand in hand and arm in arm, marching in step, left, right, left, right, coming from the direction in which we were headed, so many, we couldn't see to the end of them. They were shouting, all together, at first we couldn't make out what. Please, please let them not be Nazis, I hoped with all my hope. So did Vati. He gripped my arm. Now they were nearer. "Hail Austria," we heard, "hail to our chancellor, Kurt von Schuschnigg!"

"Inge, Inge, do you hear!" Vati's voice rang with relief and pride.

I was thrilled. I started toward them, pulling on Vati's arm. I was sure he wanted to march with them also.

He pulled me back hard. "No!" He took hold of my shoulders and made me turn around.

"But we belong with them! Why can't we march with them?"

"Inge, this is not child's play, this is serious. And I won't take chances with your safety. Don't argue with me." He pushed me along in the direction we had come from.

"What about the opera? Can't we go?"

"No. It's probably been canceled." We were coming to a small side street, and suddenly we heard noises, shouting. "Get in there, quick!" Vati pushed me into a doorway. The next moment a huge bunch of people burst out of that street just a few meters away from us and hurled themselves at the marchers. "Down with Schuschnigg!" they shouted. Vati pulled me against him. But I'd already seen fists smashing into heads and backs and bellies. And I heard the thuds of people falling down.

In a minute or two it was over. The Nazis fled. Our marchers marched on. Some who were hurt stayed behind.

"You see what can happen? Now keep close to the buildings and hurry, follow me." But suddenly Vati wheeled around. I did too. Someone was calling us. "Uncle Franz! In-ge!" The voice cracked right in the middle of my name.

"What are you doing here, trying to get yourself killed?" Vati ran. I ran too, toward someone tall and thin, a man—no, a boy, toppling forward. My father caught him in his arms. "All right, Tommi, I've got you."

Blood trickled down Tommi Löwberg's forehead. And there was blood on his mouth and his chin.

Vati had his hands full holding Tommi up, so I grabbed a handkerchief out of Vati's overcoat pocket, and I wiped Tommi's face. He had a cut over his left eyebrow, but it didn't look deep. And the blood around his mouth and chin was just from a nosebleed.

I said, "Tilt your head back." To my own surprise I sounded calm—as if I took care of people hurt in fights every day.

Tommi tilted his head back, and I held the handkerchief to his nose till the blood stopped.

"Inge, run over to Neuer Markt, find us a taxi. I'll meet you there," Vati said.

Neuer Markt was only one short block over. I ran, I waved both arms at a big black taxi, and it stopped.

My father half-dragged, half-carried Tommi to it and got him inside. I rolled the window down. My father fanned air at him and asked, "Where else besides your face are you hurt?"

"Someone kicked me in the—" He motioned where and passed out.

"Driver, hurry!" My father gave him the Löwbergs' address.

As soon as the taxi roared into motion, Tommi opened his eyes. The taxi's overhead light was still on, so I saw his eyes. They are light gray. They looked silver. And they have black rims around the irises and thick, long black eyelashes. I couldn't have ever really looked before, or I'd have noticed.

Tommi sat slumped to one side, so the first thing he saw when he regained consciousness was me looking at him.

"How do you feel?" asked my father.

"Fine, now, thank you, Uncle Franz. I'm sorry I caused you trouble."

"Don't be silly. Thank God, you're all right!" Then my father scolded him as if he were his son. "How did you dare mix yourself into something like that, when you're still only half-grown?"

"I was by far not the youngest," said Tommi proudly. "I had to be there, I'd promised some of my friends who are university students. Many of the people who marched were younger than me, really. Listen, Uncle Franz, we all have to! If we don't, it will be too late, they'll take our country away from us, they've already begun—"

"Yes!" I thought it was the bravest speech I'd ever heard.

"Shh, Tommi, calm down," said my father. "I don't suppose you told your parents where you were going?"

"No."

"I'd better prepare them. Driver, stop a moment, please." The taxi pulled over to the curb. "Wait for me, I'll be right back." Vati went into a coffeehouse to telephone.

The driver had turned off the overhead light. He sat back, lit a cigarette, and in between drags he whistled. Except for the glow of his cigarette and the dim light from a streetlamp and flashes from headlights of automobiles driving by, it was dark inside the taxi.

"My parents will be furious," said Tommi.

"But they'll be glad you didn't get hurt worse," I said.

Then neither of us said anything.

Then Tommi said, "It was certainly lucky"—he looked at me—"that your father came along just then."

I felt as let down as from a mountain peak.

"And that you came along," said Tommi.

My heart jumped around in my chest, *bumm, bumm*.

"You know something? You're nice," said Tommi. That's when he put his hand on top of mine. Just for a second. Now I know what they mean when they talk about "losing your senses." I lost mine—well, not really. They just all seemed to settle in my hand for that second, so my hand felt as if it were all of me. But it also felt like no part of me has ever felt before. As if sparks were shooting through it. As if it could burst into flames.

Then he took his hand away, and I saw everything again and heard the taxi driver whistling, a tune to which the words go: "You are my heart entire,/ Where you are not,/ I couldn't be . . ."

It's twenty hours later now. The song is still in my ears. And my hand is getting grimy. I'll have to wash it pretty soon.

(It's a good thing this book can't flip itself back to my stupid description of Tommi, which I wrote before I had any idea what he's like.)

His parents stood waiting in front of their house. Aunt Marianne pulled Tommi's head down to her and buried her face in his rumpled-up hair, then kissed him all over his face. Then she yelled at him in Viennese, "You louse-boy, you scoundrel, what colossal crust! Don't we have enough trouble already?" And tears poured down her face.

Uncle Herbert put his arm around them both.

Then Aunt Marianne pulled my father and me to them.

Passersby must have wondered why five people were huddling together like that.

"How do we thank you?" Aunt Marianne asked.

"What are friends for?" quoted my father.

When we got home, I went straight into my room so I could hug my thoughts to me, wrap them around me like a shiny cocoon.

"The poor rabbit," I heard Mutti say, "what a disappointment for her." At first I couldn't think what she meant. Oh, yes, the opera!

With so much to write about, I didn't get around to writing about the plebiscite. I'll write about that tomorrow.

Thursday, March 10

Big news: There is going to be a plebiscite. Schuschnigg gave a speech about it yesterday in Innsbruck, and everybody cheered, everybody is for it. It will be held this Sunday, March 13.

The city is all dressed up for it already, like for a festival. The

Fatherland Front people must have been working all night putting up still more bunting, flags, and streamers and sticking huge posters everywhere that say VOTE YES! YES! YES! FOR AUSTRIA! and AUSTRIA FOREVER! And more of the posters have Schuschnigg's face, a hundred times larger than life, with glittering eyeglasses and a noble, confident expression. Also, airplanes have snowed down blizzards of plebiscite leaflets—they're lying all over the sidewalks and streets, they whirl around in the wind. There's even confetti, red, white, and red. Everything's so patriotic! There's a building on the Herrengasse that used to be a private palace but is now used for offices. Well, it has two lion statues guarding the entrance, and this morning when I passed by on my way to school, both lions held Austrian flags in their mouths.

And people in the streets looked not as glum as Viennese on their way to work usually do. Lots of them smiled, and men raised their hats to passersby they didn't even know.

And—hocus-pocus!—all the anti-Semitic wall scrawls have disappeared overnight.

The police have cordoned off the whole Ringstrasse to prevent "disorders." But there aren't any Nazis around! I guess I've gotten used to seeing them with their swastikas and badges, because today on the way to school I noticed I didn't see a single one. It was uncanny. But then I thought—I guess I am an optimist—Good, they've gone to Germany, they've decided Germany's belonging to them is enough, they'll leave Austria alone.

And, I don't know if by coincidence, Herta and Brigitte, our two main-class Nazis, were absent.

Susi König thinks it's ominous. Her father, who's a correspondent for a Swiss newspaper, says the Nazis haven't just gone away but are hiding, hatching something, or else waiting for orders from Germany.

Fräulein Pappenheim didn't seem to think that. She was in a cheerful mood. She called off a test we were going to have. Instead we discussed the plebiscite. It's a very rare historical occurrence. In fact, there was never one before in the whole history of Austria. It will be a true example of democracy in action. Every grown-up Austrian will have his or her say: Yes, for a free, independent Austria. Or No, against that. But who would vote No? With the question worded the way it is, even arch-Nazis will vote as Austrians first, will vote Yes. Fräulein Pappenheim seldom tells her private opinions about anything. But she predicted that the outcome will be ninety-five, maybe even ninety-seven percent Yes. Then Hitler will know where Austria stands. So will the whole world. Then "Anschlus"—Austria annexed to Germany—will be unthinkable, out of the question!

At the end of the period we held a class plebiscite. The result was a unanimous Yes.

School let out at eleven to give students in the higher classes and teachers more time to work for the Plebiscite Committee if they wanted to.

Susi König, Anni Hopf, and I were walking down the Herrengasse when an airplane flew right over our heads. We ducked, it sounded so low. It showered another batch of plebiscite leaflets down onto rooftops, window ledges, and the street. A swarm of pigeons fluttered up with a loud *gurr, gur-*

ring. We grabbed bunches of VOTE YES leaflets and positioned ourselves at the next crossing and handed them out. Most people already had one but took another, just to be friendly.

"Good, you're home early!" Mitzi put on her new hat with the bunch of artificial cherries on top. "I have to get to the post office. When I come home from my day off, I'll have a surprise for you."

"What, Mitzi? Come on, you never get back till midnight. Tell me now!"

"I haven't got time now." She rushed out the door.

I went into her room to see if there was any evidence of anything around. She must have suspected I'd do just that. She had draped an old sheet over her sewing table and over the sewing machine. I had my fingers on a corner of the sheet and was just about to pick it up and peek, when the doorbell rang.

It was Gustl, delivering Mutti's next week's work for Huber Verlag and picking up this week's.

No sooner did I go back into Mitzi's room than the bell rang again. This time it was a delivery man with a big, long package that turned out to contain the crutches Dr. Feuerwerker ordered.

"Just in time," said Mutti, and she tried them right away. I helped her get the upholstered tops snugly under her armpits. I held my arms out, hoping I could catch her if anything went wrong.

"Look, look, I can do it, Inge!" She was as excited as a baby taking her first step. Then another step, and another and another. She hobbled from the bed toward the couch at the other end of the room. I followed right behind.

"You don't have to, Inge, I'm doing fine!" She hobbled faster. I'd never realized how wide the living room is. She was halfway back. She stopped a moment to rest. I went to her.

"No, don't help me." She made it back on her own and got back into bed exhausted but happy.

Later, when Vati came home, she came out into the hall. "Surprise!"

He took her in his arms and wanted to carry her back to bed. But she wouldn't let him.

"You're disobeying the doctor's orders," Vati scolded. "You were not supposed to try walking till next week, remember?"

Mutti laughed. "But that was before the plebiscite! I have to get into condition so I can get to the polls."

The polls will be at my old school in the Löwengasse, three blocks away.

"It's much too far, Hannelein. The Plebiscite Committee will make arrangements for people who can't get to the polls, they'll send a wheelchair."

"Not for me! I'm going there on my own two legs."

"Not if you overdo it," said Vati.

Then Oma Sofie came over with Usch and bags of food. Usch cooked supper for us. I didn't get a chance for any snooping around in Mitzi's room because it's behind the kitchen and Usch would have wanted to know what business I had in there.

Over supper, roast beef as tough as shoe leather, everyone talked about the plebiscite. Oma Sofie talked the most, perhaps because she is more used to Usch's cooking than we are and can chew it faster. She is so happy and relieved, because she has been dreading moving to Zürich, living there with Aunt Emmi, Uncle Hugo, and little Madeleine, and now, thanks to the plebiscite, she can stay in her beloved apartment amid her own things, with Usch, whom she would have missed dreadfully.

I passed up dessert (very dried-out plum cake). Now was my chance.

I went into Mitzi's room, snatched the sheet off the sewing table, and there lay my dress, shimmering in all its splendor! Carefully, carefully, in case some of it was still only basted together, I picked it up. I went to Mitzi's wardrobe. On the inside of the door is a full-length mirror. I held the dress up against me, and I looked at myself.

Suddenly Usch appeared in the mirror behind me. "I was wondering where you went just in time not to help clear the table. What's that you're holding?"

I had to tell her about the dress and all about Mitzi's wedding, whom she was marrying, and where and when.

"Hmm," Usch said, and she clicked her tongue, either at the idea of people marrying on April Fools' Day or me being the bridesmaid or both.

I put the dress back on the sewing table and put the sheet over it the way it had been.

Later

Mitzi got home earlier than usual. I was still up. She came into my room carrying a box. "Guess what's in there."

In there was the wedding dress. Her sister had sent it from Mondsee. "She wore it at her wedding. Our mother wore it. Even our grandmother wore it. Wait till you see!"

"Show it to me!"

"Are you crazy? Don't you know that's bad luck?"

"Then what's my surprise?" I pretended I didn't know.

"Come with me." She took me into her room. I pretended I hadn't gone in there before.

"See? It's done, except for the hem."

"Oh, Mitzi, it's beautiful!"

"Let's see how you look in it."

I put it on. It fits perfectly, except it's a little bit loose on top. "That's all right," Mitzi said. "You still have three weeks to fill it out."

Midnight

Then I went to bed but couldn't sleep, even though I used a method that usually works. The method is to start telling myself a story and stop at just the right point, from which point on the story continues as a dream.

This was the story:

I'm wearing the bridesmaid dress. Also, silk stockings and quite-high-heeled blue suede pumps with silver buckles. I've dabbed perfume known only to me, called Magic Nights, behind my ears and in my hair (which in the story has grown to shoulder length). I'm going to a party. (This, by the way, was not so far-fetched: Susi König is giving a party on Saturday, and she invited me. "Bring someone," she said casually, as if I knew a hundred boys who are all just waiting for me to ask them!) Anyway, the doorbell rings. It's Tommi Löwberg in an elegant dark suit and tie. The cut on his forehead still shows, a reminder of his bravery. He hands me a sprig of mimosa. Somehow he knew that's my favorite flower. His silver-gray eyes look straight into mine. Our eyes speak a better language than words. He has been thinking only, only of me, I know, he doesn't need to tell me. "We're going somewhere better than Susi König's party," he says, and takes my arm.

Next scene: We're down on the street. Tommi snaps his fingers. A fiacre appears, drawn by a shimmery stallion who looks more like a noble Lippizaner than a fiacre puller. We climb into the cab behind the driver's seat. We travel through moonlight, we come to a windswept field where a silver airplane awaits us. We climb inside. Tommi is the pilot. We rise into the air. We circle over night-shrouded Vienna, dropping down leaflets so poetically written and impassioned they will persuade all Vienna, even Seyss-Inquart, even worse Nazis than him, to vote Yes on Sunday. . . .

Well, I must have missed the stopping point.

It's really dumb, to be so superstitious, and if it weren't the middle of the night, I probably wouldn't even write this down, but I wish Schuschnigg had picked a different date. I keep thinking about the last thirteenth, what a bad day that was.

Friday, March 11

Susi König called off her party.

Mutti is flat on her back, in pain. She overdid it. She could not have made it on her own to the polls. But there won't be any polls. The plebiscite is canceled.

This morning when I went to school, the VOTE YES and Schuschnigg posters were still up, and everything looked just the same.

But then I passed a newsstand and saw headlines six centimeters high, BLOODY RIOTS IN VIENNA! AUSTRIA IN CHAOS!

I got frightened. I thought any minute I'd see fighting worse than any I've seen and maybe blood flowing in the gutters. I decided at the first sign of crowds I'd turn around, run home.

But the streets were perfectly peaceful. Nothing happened, all the way to school.

In the cloakroom Lisl Müller and Ilse Holtzer were talking about the headlines. I asked if they had seen any rioting. They hadn't.

"It's true, though," said Brigitte, coming in all excited. "The Social Democrats are trying to start a revolution!"

"Yes, just like in Russia," Gerda said.

Susi König and Anni Hopf arrived. Susi said, "*Quatsch,* that's Nazi propaganda, the Nazis are making up all those lies so then Hitler can say, Well, if Austria's in chaos, I have no choice, I'll have to march in and straighten it out."

"Your father's a Red, so your opinion doesn't count," Brigitte said. "I'll ask Fräulein Pappenheim, then you'll see."

Fräulein Pappenheim looked grim. She usually wears conservative colors, dark blue, gray, or brown. Today she was all in black.

"Fräulein Pappenheim, isn't it true that the Social Democrats are starting riots?" Brigitte asked her after roll call.

Fräulein Pappenheim has narrow lips, like two pencil lines. When she purses them, they disappear altogether. "I'm not a political commentator" was all she would say.

When it was time for English, Mr. Cookson did not appear. There is a rumor he went back to England in a hurry. Fräulein Pappenheim took over the class. Her accent in English is even worse than O.O.'s.

During Latin (we are doing Cicero's letters to Atticus) Lisl Müller got this sentence to translate: "As yet I have encountered no man who would not rather yield to Caesar's demand than fight. . . ." Frau Professor De Graaf gave a loud sniff, and we saw she had tears running down her face.

Then Frau Vollmer, Frau Direktor Waldemar's secretary, came in and announced, "Classes are being dismissed. School will be closed until further notice. You are to go to your homes as quickly as possible. Frau Direktor Waldemar wishes there to be no loitering in the streets for any reason whatsoever." Frau Vollmer went out. There was a hush, then buzzing, whispering.

Then Herta stood up on her seat, yelled, "*Juch-heh,* it's happening!" And Brigitte started shouting, "*Heil Hit—*"

Fräulein Pappenheim rapped on her desk with her pointer. "Quiet! This is still an orderly classroom! You will gather your things and leave, with decorum!"

I left with my stomach coming up into my throat, at least that's how it felt, wondering what the streets would be like and whether blood was flowing in the gutters yet.

To my huge relief Mitzi stood outside, waiting. The radio had announced that schools were closing. Mutti had sent her. I didn't have to walk home alone.

The streets were like in newsreels I have seen of Berlin and other German cities. Traffic was slowed down and in some places stopped, so many Nazis were marching, in leather boots up to their knees and brown and black uniforms, with pistols in their holsters.

"Mitzi, are those Germans? Has Germany invaded us?" I asked.

"No, those are ours, as home-grown as that mangy dog over there by the hydrant and as the fleas on his back. The Germans haven't invaded yet. But they will!" Mitzi gulped and started crying. "Listen, Schuschnigg called up the reserves! Fredl's on his way to the barracks, to his reserve regiment, and from there to God knows where. There'll be war any minute, with machine guns and poison gas and God knows what all else, giant Germany against little dwarf us, and my Fredl will be—"

"Mitzi, no!" I put my hand over her mouth.

No streetcars were running. We had to walk. Mitzi cried all the way home.

When we opened the door, there stood Fredl—in civilian clothes! "God be praised!" Mitzi yelled, and threw her arms around him. The order calling up the reserves was canceled.

"Inge, are you home?" Mutti called me in.

Vati and O.O., Oma Sofie and Usch were all here, listening to the radio. I sat down on the bed and listened too: "Latest development in the government crisis, Goering demands

Schuschnigg's resignation . . . Schuschnigg awaits word from President Miklasz . . . Barring unforeseen circumstances, capitulation is imminent . . ."

Between bulletins came music: marches and something that sounded like either Mozart or Haydn.

Then came a broadcast from down in the courtyard of the Ballhausplatz, outside the government offices. "Crowds here have swelled to the thousands," declared the announcer. A roar went up, *"Sieg Heil, Sieg Heil!"* and *"Ein Volk, ein Reich, ein Führer!"* Then came a shout, "Hang Kurt von Schuschnigg from the highest lamppost!"

That horrified me. I asked, "Could they really do that?"

Mutti nodded.

"I don't understand what's happening. Can't anybody do anything? Is the government falling?"

Everybody shushed me, another bulletin was coming.

O.O. patted the arm of his chair. I went to sit with him, and he explained: The idea of the plebiscite made Hitler furious. So during the night he sent troops to our borders, and he threatened to invade. So then Schuschnigg called off the plebiscite. But that was like giving your little finger to someone who's after both your hands, arms, and all the rest. Now Hitler wants the whole government to resign and Seyss-Inquart to take over. But President Miklasz—who's a very brave man—refuses to accept Schuschnigg's resignation. He'll have to, though. Unless Italy or England or France comes to our rescue. But O.O. doubts that they will.

"Field Marshal Goering is once again communicating with

Dr. Seyss-Inquart by telephone," said the radio, when our door-bell rang.

"Why doesn't that Mitzi of yours go see who's there?" asked Usch.

Because Fredl's here, and they have better things to do just now, I felt like telling Usch, except it's none of her business.

I went to the door.

It was Evi. "My parents don't want me to listen to the radio. They say it's not for children."

"Come listen to ours," I started to say.

"Let's go down to the courtyard," Evi said.

What a baby she is, I thought, then surprised myself—what a baby I still am sometimes! But come to think of it, why not escape from the radio and the shushing and despairing faces for a while? I said, "All right, let's."

So if anybody asks me what I was doing for at least an hour on the day that Austria died, I'll have to admit, throwing a pebble into boxes on the ground. Skipping after it, picking it up, playing Heaven and Hell with Upstairs-Evi Fried.

I didn't miss anything. The bulletin "The government has fallen" didn't come until eight in the evening.

This picture flashed into my head: President Miklasz—he has fourteen children, by the way!—and the Ministers of State, Schuschnigg, and everybody, with bullets through their chests, slumped on the pavement of the Ballhausplatz, and a brown—or black—uniformed firing squad reshouldering their guns.

That didn't happen. Nobody was shot.

The announcer said that Schuschnigg was about to make a speech.

I went to fetch Mitzi. I told her, "Come inside. You have to hear it too."

"My fellow Austrians . . ." He sounded as though he was crying! This surprised me very much. I'd never thought that people like chancellors of countries cry. He said he is giving in to the ultimatum, and he is resigning. Seyss-Inquart will be the new chancellor. Schuschnigg said he swears before the whole world that the rumors about riots and chaos and bloodshed were "false from A to Z." But lots of blood *would* be spilled if he were staying on. Then he cried right into the radio, saying, "I bid the Austrian people farewell with a heartfelt wish: May God save Austria!"

Vati went to Oma Sofie. She clutched him around the middle and laid her head against his chest. He patted her hair and her shoulders. Then he loosened her arms from around him and went to Mutti and comforted her, and then he came to me.

Oma Sofie and Usch hugged each other.

"Yessas, Maria," Mitzi sobbed, crossing herself, "what's going to happen now?"

"Quiet down, you silly girl," Usch said. "Nothing bad will happen to you."

What about to us? I wondered. I was afraid, and sad, of course, but secretly also excited. "Will there be the Anschluss now?"

Vati and O.O. answered, "Yes."

"Now will you apply for our quota numbers, Franzl?" Mutti asked.

Vati said, "Yes, now I will."

"That's the first good news I've heard all day. *Mazel tov*," said O.O.

Saturday, March 12

God didn't save Austria. Not even its name. It is called the "Ostmark" now. And it belongs to Germany.

I'm ashamed of what I wrote yesterday, about feeling secretly excited. I didn't know . . .

Something happened today that tore a hole in the world, at least that's how it felt. I couldn't have imagined it yesterday. I will write it all down very calmly, or the hole (it got patched back together) will open again, and I'll feel again as though it's swallowing me up.

This morning—I thought it was still the middle of the night, but it was really a quarter to six—the bell rang, loud and long. I heard Mitzi rushing to the door. I tiptoed to the door between my room and the hall and opened it a crack.

Three SA men in brown uniforms and black boots stood in our hall.

"*Heil Hitler, Fräulein*," they said to Mitzi. They sounded Viennese.

Mitzi rubbed her eyes and pulled her bathrobe tighter around her, and didn't greet them back.

"What's the matter, Fräulein, lost your tongue?" one joked.

"What do you want here?" she asked.

"You'll do," joked another.

"Klaus, behave yourself," said the third. "We're here on business. We want the Jew, Oskar Reichmann."

"Herr Reichmann? What for?"

I heard my father's footsteps in the hallway from the bedroom. He noticed my door open a crack and pushed it shut. I stayed still behind it and listened on.

"Are you Reichmann?" asked one of the SA men.

"No. He's asleep. I'm his son-in-law. Perhaps I can help," my father answered politely.

"Certainly you can. Get your clothes on, get your toothbrush. But Reichmann has to 'help' too, so wake him up. If you don't, we will."

Mutti was awake now, knocking on my wall, calling me. I went in to her by the door from my room to the living room. I told her what I'd seen and heard. I asked, "Mutti, where are they taking them? When will they be back?"

Mutti shook her head. Maybe never. She didn't say it, but I read it on her face.

"Va—" I started to scream. She put her hand over my mouth. My teeth chattered. She pulled me into her bed. I curved myself against her. She felt warm. But I'd been shaking, and I couldn't stop.

We heard Vati knocking on the study door. "Oskar, wake up!"

Then Vati came in to us. He was dressed as though he were going to work. He said, "Don't worry. They're taking us to clean some streets, that's all." He kissed Mutti, then me. "We'll be back soon."

O.O. looked in. He had dressed as formally as he would for

going to temple. He said, "We will be all right, I promise you." He waved and shut the door.

Then we heard the outside door close.

Then Mutti crumpled up her pillow and hit it with her fists and said into the pillow in a strangled whisper, "They will not come back. We'll never see them again."

She sobbed so hard, the bed shook. I felt like I was in a nightmare, falling, as though the bed with us in it were falling down the hole. At the same time I felt very angry, like shaking her and screaming, *You be the mother, you comfort me!*

For a moment I thought maybe I did scream it, because she turned to me, not sobbing anymore, trying to get herself under control. "Hand me my cigarettes and lighter, would you?"

I handed them to her. She pulled a cigarette out of the pack, struck a flame, puffed—and seemed herself again. "Inge, pretend you didn't see me like that. They will be back. Of course they will."

Mitzi came in. "*Gnä' Frau, Gnä' Frau,* to think *I* opened the door—" She mopped her face with her apron.

"You had to. You can't blame yourself for that. Now help me to the bathroom."

Mutti got washed, dressed; I did too.

Then Mitzi brought us breakfast.

We put lumps of sugar in our coffee cups, we stirred, we spread butter and apricot jam on our slices of bread, to have something to do.

"Inge, switch on the radio."

". . . today marks the homecoming of Adolf Hitler to the land

116

of his birth," said the announcer, sounding overjoyed. "In the Führer's little native town of Braunau-am-Inn throngs of well-wishers stand, prepared to wait for him all day if need be, their arms full of flowers, their hearts full of love. And everywhere throughout the Ostmark the populace heaves sighs of relief that thanks to the might of the Führer's armed services, the SA and SS, disorder and bloodshed have been averted; calm is restored, jubilation reigns—"

"Turn it off!" Mutti swung herself out of bed. "Hand me my crutches. I'm going to make some telephone calls."

"Whom will you call?" I followed her into the study.

"Whoever might know something. The police, first. After all, we are still citizens, we haven't been deprived of our rights yet. What happened may not be legal, we'll see." She lit another cigarette and dialed. "Hello, kindly connect me with the police." She sounded confident. While she waited, she asked me, "Would you bring me my address book? It's in the little drawer of the table by my bed."

That drawer is also where she keeps her packs and packs of Memphis cigarettes and her many lighters.

I took out the address book. I also took out a pack already open. I pulled a cigarette out. I tapped it on the back of my hand the way Mutti does. I stuck it in my mouth. I thought, Whatever it does for her, it can do the same for me. I turned the tiny metal wheel of one of the lighters. The flame shot up, blue on the bottom, yellow on top. I held the cigarette to the flame, and I puffed. It lit! I blew out a mouthful of smoke—like a smoker! I puffed again. I let the smoke flow and float around inside my mouth, under my tongue, blew it out again, thinking, There!

But my mother doesn't just blow the smoke around in her mouth. She takes it down into her throat. I tried that. It didn't work, my throat closed up as if there were a gate to it. I forced it open. I breathed down a gulp of smoke. It tasted like a dung heap smells. No, worse. I gagged. I coughed and coughed. I thought I would never get rid of the taste.

The cigarette smoldered, its ash fell on the floor, it nearly burned my fingers. I stubbed it out in the ashtray. Just then Mitzi came in. "Rotten beast! What are you doing? I ought to kick you clear across this room! I will, next time you try it!"

It sounds crazy, but Mitzi's yelling like that seemed like the first normal thing all day, and I felt like hugging her for it.

"Where's that address book?" Mutti called.

Soon she hobbled back in. She was done telephoning. The police had said they were sorry, they couldn't do anything. And Vati and O.O. weren't the only ones. She had found out that SA men had come for Max Plattau's brother and old Herr Grossbart and Rabbi Taglicht too. At Max Plattau's brother's apartment they had ransacked drawers and cabinets and had carried away the silver and other things.

"Thank God they didn't do that here," said Mitzi.

Mutti shrugged. "Things are only things."

After a while Uncle Herbert came over. He batted his arms at the smoke in the room and threw the window open wide. He put his arms around Mutti and scolded her for smoking like such a chimney.

"Oh, Herbert, Herbert!" Now that he was here, she let herself go. "I'm so afraid! They made them bring their toothbrushes, and you know where people with toothbrushes get sent!"

"Hannerl, stop. Don't imagine things worse than they are. They're bad enough. Franz was right. The fact is, they are forcing Jewish men, also some women, to clean streets. I saw some with my own eyes on my way over here. And some of those people had to use toothbrushes. That's the SA's idea of a joke."

He sat on her bed and stroked her hand and made her stay still a few minutes and not smoke.

Mutti told me to go ask Mitzi to make some coffee.

"No, I don't have time," Uncle Herbert said.

"Oh, Herbert, what are we going to do without you?" Mutti said with a sort of moan, as though he were leaving forever.

Don't be silly, I was sure he'd say, or something like that. And he did say, "I'll see you tomorrow." But only after a moment. And during that moment he looked terribly sad.

Then he wiped that look off his face and put a grin on it. "Have you heard the latest?" And he told the oldest Count Bobby joke there is, the one in which Count Bobby, the addle-brained nobleman, pours a bowl of spinach over his head, and when his friend asks, "But, Bobby, why are you pouring spinach over your head?" he answers, "Oh, dear me, I thought it was noodle soup!"

"No, we never heard that one," I said, which was almost more of a joke than the joke. And we managed to laugh a little bit.

Then he had to leave. I went to the door with him. He put his hands on my shoulders. He said, "Your father and grandfather will be all right." He sounded as though he believed it. But he still looked very sad.

I asked him, "Uncle Herbert, do you know something you're not telling me?"

"Yes. But it's not about them, so don't worry."

I begged him to tell it to me. But he didn't have time. He said I'd know soon enough.

How did we get through the rest of the day? We played games: my old animal lotto, even though neither of us could win because three cards—the hippopotamus, zebra, and cockatoo cards—are missing. Then checkers. And the game of imitating our normal looks and voices. Not pick up sticks. Mutti said her fingers weren't steady enough. "I'll tell you what, I'll teach you chess."

But I couldn't learn. My mind refused to let in new things like chess rules. It was too busy shutting things out, like, Where *do* they send people when they make them bring their toothbrushes? I really knew, or thought I knew, the answer: to Dachau. Dachau is a concentration camp. What that means, I don't exactly know. But I have heard that people don't come back from there. . . .

At ten minutes to six O.O. and Vati came home. For the first second I didn't recognize them. I thought they were two old beggars. Then I threw myself around Vati's neck and hugged him so hard, he said, "Stop, you're knocking me down."

Their coats were rumpled and splattered with mud. O.O.'s hat was bashed in, someone had stepped on it. O.O. was stooped over, like a ninety-year-old man. Vati's eyes were red and swollen, he could hardly see out of them. His hands shook. His mouth quivered when he spoke.

The reason the SA men had come looking for O.O. is, they had gotten hold of a list from the Jewish Community of people who had contributed money to the Plebiscite Committee.

They had shoved O.O. and my father into a truck full of Jews. They drove them to the Seitenstette, where the temple is. Especially many plebiscite posters had been put up on the walls of the buildings there. They made them tear the posters down with their fingernails and scrub the paste off the walls, then scrub the sidewalks and street. Uncle Herbert was right, part of the time they made them use toothbrushes, for a joke. They sloshed bucketfuls of ammonia and other stuff that burns the skin and stings the eyes over the street and laughed when "by accident" they also sloshed the scrubbers' hands and sometimes their faces. O.O., Rabbi Taglicht, my father, and some others thought that as long as they were scrubbing, they might as well try to scrub away the JEWS, GO CROAK scrawls they had uncovered by stripping the posters away. So they started to. But the paint would not come off. And the SA men hit them and kicked them and ordered them back to scrubbing the street. The most shocking thing to my father was how many people, whole crowds, came to watch the spectacle and joked and jeered, and not one said a word against it. "Excuse me," said my father in the middle of telling this, and rushed into the bathroom.

"You know what Rabbi Taglicht said while scrubbing? 'I am cleaning God's earth.' And that's what we were all doing," said O.O. Then his eyes fell shut and he went to sleep, right where he was sitting, on the couch near the stove, with his overcoat still on.

After a while Vati took off O.O.'s shoes. And I covered him with the lap rug we keep at the foot of that couch. It's made of plush and feels like fur. O.O. stayed asleep, snoring regularly.

Sunday, March 13

During the night O.O. moved into the study. This morning he and Vati both got up late and looked better and were so hungry, they ate twice as much for breakfast as usual.

At eleven o'clock Uncle Herbert called up. He spoke to Vati.

"The Löwbergs will be here in fifteen minutes," said Vati, coming from the telephone.

"How come?" I asked. They never visit on a Sunday morning.

"To say good-bye. They're going away."

So that's what Uncle Herbert meant!

Clang! Mutti smashed a weight into the bed frame and used a word she hardly ever uses.

"Hannerl, Hannerl, that won't change anything," said Vati. "Inge, come into the kitchen."

My father never sets foot in there! He doesn't even know how to make coffee or boil an egg.

But now he went, and I followed him. He took a loaf of bread out of the bread box. "Where's a board to cut this on? And where's a knife?"

I gave him both. He started slicing bread for sandwiches. "The Löwbergs have to catch a train at twelve thirty. They didn't have anything in the house to make a lunch with. I said we'd fix them something."

"Where are they going?"

"To Zagreb." That's in Yugoslavia.

"For how long?"

"For good."

"How come?"

"Well, Uncle Herbert has a cousin there who's also a doctor and can help him find work in a hospital."

"What about his patients and everything here? How come they're doing this all of a sudden? They're not even Jewish, at least Aunt Marianne isn't."

"It's very complicated. Look, Ingelein, I'm very bad at explaining things like that, don't make me. See if there's any salami and cheese from yesterday. And do we have any mustard?"

As I was looking for those things, Mitzi came back. She wasn't taking this whole Sunday off, she'd only been to church. "*Yessas*, Herr Dornenwald! What are you doing in my kitchen?" She wouldn't have been more surprised if she'd seen an elephant standing there holding a bread knife with his left foot. "Let *me* do that!"

"Gladly." Vati asked her to fix sandwiches of whatever we had and wrap up whatever else there was, fruit, cake, anything, to make a lunch for three.

"Oh, Herr Dornenwald, no! You aren't, you can't be . . . ?"

"No, no, we're not going anywhere. It's for the Löwbergs. Inge, give Mitzi a hand." He went out.

Mitzi rummaged in the icebox, I reached up to a shelf for the mustard jar. It slipped out of my hand and fell and broke.

"Clumsy beast! Help like that I don't need. Do me a favor, get out of my kitchen!" Mitzi screamed in earnest, really furiously.

"I've seen *you* drop things and smash things plenty of times!" I broke into tears and got out of "her kitchen."

Then they came. Only for ten minutes, said Uncle Herbert. Their taxi was waiting down on the street. They didn't even take their coats off.

Vati and I had both gone to the door. Vati took Uncle Herbert and Aunt Marianne in to my mother.

That left Tommi and me standing in our hall together. "Come into my room," it took me a long moment to work up the courage to say.

He sat on the edge of my desk. I sat on my bed. I stared down at my bedspread as if I'd never seen it before. I wanted it to turn into a real field of real flowers. I wanted to be sitting next to Tommi in the train, looking out the window at real fields— not that poppies, daisies, or cornflowers ever really bloom in March.

"How come you're leaving so suddenly?"

"Because my father may lose his job any minute and be put in jail or in a concentration camp, and my mother may go crazy, and I might wring the neck of whoever is—" He pounded his fist on my desk.

"Whoever is what, Tommi?"

"Writing hate letters to my mother. She's been getting one every day. With swastikas on top, skulls and bones at the bottom, and disgusting stuff in between."

"Like what?"

"Oh, that my father is a Communist agitator, that he organizes riots, that he is a butcher with a scalpel. It would be funny if it weren't so vile. He's always been a Social Democrat. And he doesn't do operations, he never uses scalpels! 'Divorce him,' say the letters, 'or else . . .' And then come the threats. First my mother ignored the whole thing. Then she got annoyed, then frightened. She went to the police. But the officer just shrugged and said, '*Gnädige Frau,* in your position, what can you expect, nowadays?'

"And her parents—my grandparents, whom I used to adore"—Tommi's voice cracked, he had to clear his throat— "they're just as bad! You know, when I was little, they used to take me with them on vacations, to Baden, to Ischl. They showed me off to everybody, they were so proud of me, and I, of them. I thought they were so elegant, almost like nobility. They want her to divorce him! Then she and I would live with them, and they would graciously 'close their eyes' to my being half Jewish." He crossed the room and stood over me. "Inge, I'm sorry. It's very ugly. I shouldn't have told you."

His standing so near made me dizzy. "Yes, you should," I mumbled.

He tipped my chin up. "I hope I see you again."

Then our parents came in, Mutti too, on her crutches. Not one of them had a dry face.

We all went into the hall. The grown-ups kissed. Uncle Herbert and Aunt Marianne kissed me too.

Tommi and I shook hands. We said *"Tschüss"* to each other. And just like in my story, our eyes knew another language. At least I think they did.

Vati went with them to see them off.

I wanted to, but also not to, in case I might say something childish-sounding on the way that would spoil the grown-up good-bye we'd already said, and not said.

Besides, as the Löwbergs were leaving, Mutti said to me, "Remember that day we went to Schönbrunn? I feel the way you did then."

Sure, I remembered, and how nice they'd been to me. So it was only right that now I should stay home with her.

We talked about good-byes and people leaving. I asked whether, when we leave, we might go to Yugoslavia too.

"We'd have to get visas first, and that's not easy."

"Did the Löwbergs?"

"No. Non-Jews don't have to."

"But I thought Uncle Herbert was Jewish."

"By birth. By conviction he's not religious, just like we aren't. But he got baptized, just before he married Aunt Marianne. Because it meant so much to her parents to have the ceremony performed by a priest, in a church."

Monday, March 14

A priest, a church—those are why Mitzi is in such a foul mood.

Today when I came into the kitchen, she stuck my breakfast in front of me without a smile or a good morning.

Then she muttered, "Today comes the Devil to Vienna."

I dropped my whole *Kipferl* into my cup. Coffee sloshed over the table. "You snooped!" I accused her. "You read that in my book!"

"What are you, crazy? I didn't read that in any book! Everybody knows it! Today Hitler's coming, that's who! Look what you did, clumsy thing." She grabbed a rag and wiped the table with her left hand (she's left-handed). So then I saw that her ring finger was bare.

"Mitzi, where's your diamond ring?"

"In its box. I'm giving it back. *If* I ever see Fredl again."

"How come? What do you mean?"

"Because *I'm* no heathen, I'm getting married in a church or nowhere."

"What happened?"

She told me: They had a fight.

Fredl is not as religious as she and likes to do other things Sunday mornings. But yesterday he went to church with her. After all, their banns for the wedding were already up, it wouldn't have looked right for him not to be there.

Well, when they got to the Kolodnitz Church, a big swastika flag flew from the entrance. And Fredl said, "I'm not going in."

"Yes, you are." Mitzi pulled him in.

But he didn't stay long.

The priest said in his sermon that Cardinal Innitzer had promised that all good Viennese Catholics would be for the Anschluss of Austria to Germany and would welcome Hitler to Vienna.

"Not this good Viennese Catholic," Fredl said. "They can kiss my good Catholic—" and he walked out.

He waited for her outside, and he told her he'd never set foot in there again. Or in any church with a swastika flying.

"Then where will we get married?" Mitzi asked. "In a beer hall?"

"Fine with me."

"Well, not with me!" Mitzi had torn away from him and started running. And Fredl hadn't followed.

"Oh, Mitzi, that's awful," I said. "You have to make up."

"Oh, you, you're just worried you won't get to wear your fancy bridesmaid's dress!"

I was very hurt by that, and I got out of her way.

I went in to Mutti. She sat in bed working, surrounded by piles of manuscripts.

I turned the radio on. ". . . strewing flowers along the route the Führer's open car and the accompanying vehicles are expected to take," it blared. "Our children and our children's children will read in the history books of the future about this never-to-be-forgotten triumphal day."

My mother retched. "Turn that off."

I did. "When will they get here?"

"How should I know?"

"I feel cooped up, Mutti. I want to go for a walk."

"Are you crazy? On a day like today Jews stay home."

"Then why is Vati out? Where did he go, anyway?"

"To the Plattaus'."

"How come? Doesn't he see Herr Plattau enough at the office?"

"Don't be fresh. Haven't you got any homework?"

"No."

"Then look through this manuscript for me." She handed me a thick folder of three hundred partly typed, partly illegibly handwritten pages about life at the Court of Emperor Franz Joseph. "See if all the pages are in order and if every chapter has a heading."

Then the telephone rang. O.O. was in the study and answered it. It was a very short conversation. In a moment he came in to us. "Inge, that was for you."

"Who was it? Why didn't you call me?"

"It was someone named Anni Hopf. She said I shouldn't. She wants you to meet her on the Stefansplatz."

"You're not going," Mutti said.

I headed for the study. "I'll call her back."

"Don't," O.O. said. "She doesn't want you to. She said especially that you shouldn't."

Hmm, that was odd. Anni Hopf calls me up so seldom, I'd have thought that when she does, she'd want to be called back. Then it occurred to me that maybe her parents wouldn't want her going anywhere either today (they are not Jewish but very much against the Nazis). Well, probably she didn't want them to know— yes, that must be it. I decided she and Susi König had a plan to meet and go someplace from where they could have a good view of the "open car and accompanying vehicles" arriving in Vienna. I couldn't get over how nice it was of them to want me along.

I handed Mutti back the manuscript about the Emperor Franz Joseph. "I'll read this later. Can I go up to Evi's awhile?"

"All right."

I went the shortest way to the Inner City. It was all decked out, but differently.

When I was little and we still had Kaethe, she once took me along to the cinema, to a film called *Frau Schmidt, Frau Braun*. Frau Schmidt wore proper, demure clothes and was married to an undertaker. Frau Braun wore gaudy, flirty clothes, and she drank lots of schnapps and was married to a tavern keeper. Aside from their clothes they looked so much alike, I asked if they were twins. Kaethe said yes. But later I figured it out. They weren't twins. They were one and the same woman. Just with two different husbands.

That's what Vienna today reminded me of.

The posters with Schuschnigg's face and VOTE YES FOR AUSTRIA were gone. And—hocus-pocus!—the JEWS, KICK THE BUCKET and JEWS, GO CROAK scrawls were back on the walls. From other walls and from kiosks Hitler's face stared down, eyes as big as soup tureens. The red-white-red bunting and flags were gone, replaced by red-white-black ones and swastikas. And everywhere were uniforms. Whoever wasn't wearing one at least had a swastika badge or pin. And children clutched little swastika flags in their hands.

I kept my eyes to myself. And I headed for the Stefansplatz.

It's a rather small square, you can walk around it in less than ten minutes, so there wasn't too much chance of my missing Anni Hopf. Still, I thought it was odd that she hadn't said on which side of the square she'd be.

From the giant main portal of St. Stephen's fluttered three swastika flags.

I walked around to the back. I stood at the far end of the square, craning my head back, looking up and up, past the gargoyles, past the turrets to the tip of the tower, where the old double eagle scratches the clouds.

"It's a wonder it doesn't come crashing down on our heads," I heard a voice say behind me.

Three

I turned around. And everything turned around with me. The whole world took an extra whirl. Toward me came Lieselotte, holding out her hand.

St. Stephen's tower crashing down—something like that would have had to happen to keep me from taking her hand.

She had grown about three centimeters. Her old green loden coat was too short for her. Under it she wore an old dress I remembered, with daisies. And her hair—she'd had it cut, not really short, but shorter than it used to be.

I tugged at it. "Now you'll never be able to sit on it!"

"That's true."

The things people say after not seeing each other for so long! We laughed. And we put our arms around each other.

While we were hugging I felt something cool and moist touching my ankle. I looked down. It was a snout. It belonged to a long reddish-brown dog with short legs. I said, "He looks just like the dog on a picture postcard I got—I *thought* it was from you!"

"It was! I wanted to show you what I got for Christmas! Schnackerl, look"—she picked him up—"that's her, that's Inge!"

She held him out to me. I shook his paw. "He's beautiful."

"Oh, Inge, it worked, you got my message!"

"What message? There wasn't any on the card—"

"I know. I mean now, on the telephone."

"No. Just Anni Hopf called. She said I should meet her."

"That was me! That was the message! Oh, Inge, it's really you, and here we really are!" We grabbed each other and spun around together like in a dance till Schnackerl's leash got twisted around our legs and he barked and we nearly tripped.

She disentangled the leash. She said, "Mutterl and I got back the night before last, really late. Heinz and Papa have been here two weeks already. We have a telephone in our new apartment, I couldn't wait to call you! But I didn't dare. It's in the hall, someone's always going by. Finally, this afternoon, they all went out, so at last I could call. Of course I couldn't say it was me, and I didn't dare wait for you to come to the telephone. My father could have come back any second, and if he'd caught me—" The sentence dangled in the air like a curtain.

Lieselotte jerked her hand as if she were shoving it out of the way. "Listen, I have so much to tell you. We live on the Schwedenplatz now, right near here, in a beautiful apartment, wait till you—" *See it,* she was going to say, but of course I wouldn't be going there. "And I'm coming back to Herrengasse Gymnasium. Oh, Inge, I still can't believe it!"

"Me either!"

"But it's true!"

We jumped into the air, like little girls again.

"But, Lieselotte, how come you sent me that picture postcard from Regensburg? What were you doing there? And how come you printed my address instead of writing it and didn't write a single word on the card?"

We hadn't taken our eyes off each other's faces. Now she looked down at the sidewalk. "I went to a youth rally there. With my Jungmädel troop. I did write you about that, but—" Something happened in her face. I can't describe it. I can only describe how it made me feel: shy with her, as I never was before. Afraid of saying something wrong.

"I wrote you lots of letters," Lieselotte said, still not looking at me.

"I didn't get them."

"I know. You still will. Don't ask me about that now. Please!"

"All right. But did you get my letter, that I sent care of your school?"

"And how!" She laughed her old laugh. She clapped her hand to her forehead. "Did that ever land me in the soup!"

Then we had to hold our ears because up in the tower the St. Stephen's bells started ringing. "Four o'clock! Schnackerl, come!" She pulled on his leash. "I still have to change into my uniform. I have to go strew flowers at You-know-who." She grabbed my hand.

"Come, walk with me part of the way. It's on your way home."

I would have anyway, even if it had been ten kilometers out of my way. We swung hands and walked fast. My barette clasp came undone. My hair hung over my eyes. I stuck it back behind my ear.

"*Heh,* your hair's longer! Is your mother finally letting you let it grow?" Lieselotte asked.

"No. She just can't drag me to the barbershop as easily as she used to." I told her about Mutti's accident. And I realized one of the things I've missed the most was the way Lieselotte can listen.

Then she asked, "How's Mitzi?"

I told her that Mitzi and Fredl were going to get married on April Fools' Day, but that they'd had a fight.

"What about?"

I told her that too.

Then we heard marching, some SA men came goosestepping along, and I thought, Somebody like Lieselotte's father could get someone like Fredl into bad trouble. I said, "Don't tell what I just told you to anybody, all right?"

"Naturally not." Her eyebrows knitted together. She was thinking, hard. "Listen, I'll tell you something if you—"

"Promise not to tell? Of course. What?"

She shook her head. "No, I can't. I mustn't."

By then we were at the Schwedenplatz. Lieselotte stopped. She pointed to a house opposite. "That's where we live, on the fourth floor. See those windows? You can look out and see over the whole square—" She stepped in front of me, to hide me.

"Just in case your father's looking?"

"Yes."

"What would he do, Lieselotte?"

"Put me on the next train back to Munich." She tried to make it sound like a joke. But it sounded serious.

"How come he's letting you go back to Herrengasse Gymnasium? I mean, he could have just made you go to a different school."

"I promised him I wouldn't—oh, you know."

I knew: be friends with me. I didn't know what to say.

"Inge, listen, let's not keep bringing up stuff like that. We don't have to, you'll understand it all when I . . . you'll see. Look, through the entrance to that building is a little courtyard. Let's go in there a minute."

In the courtyard we were out of view. There was even a bench. We sat down a moment.

"Inge, listen, I'll tell you the thing I was going to, only swear you won't tell a soul except Mitzi. And she can tell Fredl."

"I swear."

Lieselotte knows a church without a swastika flag. At least it didn't have one yesterday, when she was there.

Secret though I keep this book, I won't write down the church's name or where it is.

Then Lieselotte reached into her pocket. "Here." She handed me a schilling. "I owe you this."

"What for?"

"Don't you remember? Or did you already get yours too?"

Then I remembered. "Not yet. Congratulations!"

"Thanks. Now I have to go." She and Schnackerl started running. "Can you meet me tomorrow?" she called over her shoulder. "I'll be there around eleven."

I knew where she meant: at the church.

"Yes," I called.

On my way home, though the streets were just as full of jubilant Nazis, and Hitler's car was probably already almost in Vienna, I felt as happy as a—I can't think of anything happy enough to be a good comparison.

I smiled to myself, I skipped, I hummed, I stopped at the nearest flower stand. With the schilling from Lieselotte I bought a big bunch of narcissus for Mutti in case she was angry I'd stayed "at Evi's" so long.

When I got home, I rushed straight into the kitchen. "Mitzi, you'll never guess what—"

"Shh, you heartless thing, don't shout so!"

"All right, you grouch, I *won't* tell you. You'll be sorry!" I stuck the flowers in a vase and went into the living room.

Mutti lay still, on her back. Vati sat on the bed, his head in his hands. O.O. sat slumped over the table. Nobody turned or looked up. Nobody said a word.

"Mutti, look, I bought these for you. I didn't see why only Hitler should be getting flowers today."

I hoped that would make them smile. It didn't. I saw now they were crying, all three.

"What happened?" I asked.

Vati shook his head.

Mutti said, "Max Plattau died."

When you hear something like that, at first it's just words, it doesn't sink in. "Vati's business partner?" I asked stupidly. "But I thought you were visiting him!"

"I was," he said in a flat voice. "Then I left, and he did it."

"Did what?"

O.O. said, "This is one thing I don't think Inge has to know."

Vati nodded.

"I don't see how we can keep it from her," said my mother. "Ingelein, he killed himself. They sent his brother to Dachau. Max couldn't bear it. He thought he might be next."

"How did he do it?"

"He jumped."

They live—I mean, lived—in the High House, a modern building, nine stories high. On the top floor.

I pictured him hitting the sidewalk.

"Inge, come." My father pulled me onto his lap. Like a baby. But I couldn't not sit there.

He put his cheek against my hair and rocked back and forth with me and thought out loud, "Poor Maxl, poor Maxl."

"Franz, you did all you could," my mother said.

"I know. I talked myself hoarse, I told him a hundred reasons why he shouldn't. But the only good reason"—Vati tightened his arms around me—"poor Max didn't have."

"Franzl, don't," my mother said.

"Yes, I have to say it. It's important, Inge should know it."

I knew what he was going to say before he said it: "The only good reason is being a father. Having someone like you."

Like me? Who, until I came into this room, was as happy as the Queen of the May because my best friend is back, whose father is an SA man?

I felt sick. I got off my father's lap.

Now it's very late at night. I haven't been able to sleep. Every time I closed my eyes, I saw Max Plattau hurtling through the air. I couldn't shut that picture out, and I couldn't switch off my thoughts. Meantime I was twisting the Mogen Dovid around on my necklace. (I'd forgotten to take it off before I went to bed.) I must have twisted pretty hard. Finally the necklace broke.

So I got up and put it in its box. I hope Herr Fried can fix it. Then I wrote all this. And now I don't want to get back into my bed and have those thoughts the rest of the night. . . .

Tuesday, March 15

Mitzi sleeps like a bear in a winter cave. I had to knock a really long time before she opened her door.

I said, "Mitzi, I couldn't sleep."

"Come in, then," she said.

Her bed is narrower but softer than mine, and her eiderdown is overstuffed and extra warm.

On the wall alongside the bed is a little wooden crucifix with nails through Christ's hands and feet, and blood painted on. It looks very real.

But over her headboard is a cheerful picture of the Virgin Mary in a sky-blue cloak with long, blond wavy hair and a halo of golden stars. "I already prayed for poor Herr Plattau, but again won't hurt." Mitzi got on her knees to the picture. "Holy Mother of God, in spite of what he's done, don't let his poor soul be damned for all eternity. And don't forget, find a good Catholic way for me to marry my Fredl. Amen."

Then she turned the light off and lay down.

"Listen, Mitzi, I know a church with no swastika flag. At least it didn't have one yesterday."

"Go on. Where is it, up in Heaven?"

"No. Can you keep a secret?"

"Haven't I kept plenty for you in my time?"

"Yes, but this one is more serious. If you tell, something terrible could happen."

"You can trust me," Mitzi said.

So I told her the name of the church. And that I was going there in the morning and that she could come with me and see for herself.

So then she wanted to know how I knew about it. And I said, "Lieselotte's back. She told me."

Mitzi sat up. The moon shone in, and I could see how happy she looked. She got out of bed, knelt down on the floor, and said, "Thank you, Holy Mother of God."

She came back into bed and sighed and said, "It just goes to show, when the whole world turns into a stinking dung heap, here and there a flower pokes through."

"That's beautiful, Mitzi! That's like a poem!"

"Go on. Poems don't have dung heaps in them. And don't hog the whole pillow." She pulled the pillow over and the over-stuffed eiderdown up to our chins, and we went to sleep.

Later

But it didn't work out as we'd planned. I couldn't go.

Mutti was very upset, because Herr Plattau's funeral was this morning, and she tried to keep Vati and O.O. from going to it. She said, "Wasn't Saturday enough for you? Don't you know the Nazis are rampaging out there? They've already arrested six thousand Jews since Friday night. And today Hitler makes a big speech. In honor of that they'll grab themselves a few thousand more, and where more conveniently than at a Jewish funeral? Father?" She caught hold of O.O.'s arm. "You didn't even know Max that well, you don't have to go. You shouldn't even still be here, you should be on a boat for New York. Oh, I know, you're waiting to see me on my feet. Well, look—" She stood up for a moment, freely, without support.

Vati quickly grabbed her and put a crutch under her arm. He said, "We're going. We'll be careful." He took it for granted I'd stay with Mutti. Under the circumstances I couldn't refuse.

So only Mitzi went to the church.

Vati and O.O. came home from the funeral sad but safe.

When Mitzi came home, *she* was happy as a May queen, I could already tell by the sound of her opening the front door.

I went into the hall. "Well, is it true what I told you?"

"Yes! And everything's on again, it's all set!" The ring was back on her finger. She flashed it at me. Then she grabbed me and lifted me off the floor as though I were a lot smaller than her (I'm not, I only weigh less). "Look what I brought you!"

She set me down and gave me a box, the kind they sell at country fairs, with a design of alpine flowers burnished into the wood. It was tied shut with a blue ribbon. Folded inside were the letters Lieselotte wrote me while she was in Munich.

Midnight

I've read them so many times I know them almost by heart. Now, before I go to sleep, I'll put them in here:

Wednesday, November 10, 1937

Dear Inge,

It's hard to believe that was me who wrote you yesterday, about Scholz-Klink and all the people I have to say *Heil Hitler* to, and that it was only yesterday. It feels more like a few years ago, so much has happened in the meantime.

For instance, remember our bet? Well, now I owe you a schilling.

I started this letter to you in my head while tramping the last few kilometers back to the place where the buses picked us up. It was the longest hike of my life. I've never been so tired! But before I go to sleep, I want to put all this down while it's still fresh in my mind.

We started out at seven thirty this morning, all the Jungmädel troops of Munich, hundreds and hundreds, maybe a thousand girls. And our troop was picked to be first! It was a shiny morning, really, like in that poem we had to memorize last year, "How splendidly all nature shines/ How laughs the sun, etc.," remember?

I felt happy, how could anyone not on such a day? The only thing missing was your company. So I imagined that instead of Karla Hildebrandt, you were marching next to me. I imagined you in a white shirt, necktie, blue pleated skirt, wind jacket, and hiking boots, with a pack on your back, singing the songs, keeping step, fitting in. I thought, That would show them! Then they'd know what *Quatsch* that is, the stuff they say about Jews.

It's everywhere. Even in little children's picture books! Like, for instance, last night I was putting Uta Pfaltz to bed. She's only five, she can't really read yet, but she started to "read" me her favorite story: "See, Lieselotte, here are all the Aryan children, standing by the classroom door. They're laughing, they're happy. This boy is saying, '*Etsch, etsch,* you can't stay in our school,' to those others. Because they're the Jews. See their kinky hair and their big crooked noses that look like number sixes and big lips, and they're sticking out their tongues, ugh! The teacher is throwing them out—"

"Uta, *pfui!*" I shut the book.

"Don't you like it?"

"No!" I started reading her another one, about a boy named Peter flying to the moon on the back of a June bug. I said, "That's a lot more believable."

Uta laughed. She thought I was joking.

Inge, maybe I shouldn't write you things like that. But I'm too tired to stop myself. Those things are on my mind so much, and there is no one here I can talk about them with.

Anyway, this morning we hiked south to the Starnberger See. That's in the same direction as

Austria. The farther south we got, the more beautiful it was. I said to Karla, "These woods and mountains can't know they're across the border, they look exactly like on the other side." And the river sparkled, the air was like perfume of evergreen, the path was crinkly with fallen leaves and soft with pine and hemlock needles. Just when I thought things couldn't get any lovelier, there was a *whoosh* and a big hawk soared up from a branch right over our heads! It was so close, I saw its white-and-brown-speckled breast and reddish tail-feathers! Remember, one Sunday when we were little, your father took us to the Natural History Museum, and we looked at a whole roomful of glass cases with different birds of prey inside? Well, it's even more thrilling when you see one in the wild. I watched it rise up and up till it dwindled to a tiny dot in the blue and I couldn't see it anymore.

Then something else thrilling happened—at least I thought then it was thrilling: Irmgard Knauer came all the way back from the head of the line to talk to me. She's our troop leader. No matter what you'd think of her, you'd have to admit she's beautiful. She has a figure like an actress. Her hair is the color of wheat (not dyed). Her complexion is all pink and white, and natural too, not out of rouge and powder pots. Everybody in the troop admires her like mad. And Karla told me lots of girls have crushes on her.

Irmgard asked what I'd been looking at. I told her. She was impressed. She said jokingly she couldn't tell a hawk from a hen, even up close. And she invited me to march in the front with her so we could have a talk.

"You're so lucky," whispered Karla. And other girls looked at me enviously. Only, not Edeltraut. I forgot to tell you, Edeltraut Wiecks, my enemy, was marching very first in line, head high, back ramrod-straight, chest out, like a newsreel soldier. It was her turn to carry the flag. So naturally she didn't turn around. But she knew I was there, she could hear Irmgard talking to me.

Irmgard told me all the different events coming up for our troop: a folk-song evening, a special showing of the Olympics film, a dance, and she said, "If we're lucky, we may be asked to attend a giant youth rally in Regensburg, all expenses paid. You know who might be there?" Her voice went fluttery. "Magda Goebbels!" Magda Goebbels is supposed to be the most beautiful woman in the whole Reich. She is Irmgard's ideal.

Then she told about her boyfriend, Otto, how handsome he is and how much she misses him. He's doing his year of Land Service on a farm in Schleswig-Holstein. He has already asked her to marry him four times. She hopes she will be able to. The only reason she might not would be if he doesn't get into the SS. Because Irmgard is in Faith and Beauty, and Faith and Beauty girls are supposed to marry only SS men.

"Do you have any boyfriends yet?" she asked me. Of course you know what I answered. So then she looked me up and down and down and up and said, "Don't worry, you will soon. Our Munich boys have good taste." And she said she wouldn't be surprised if when I'm fourteen and get promoted into the B.D.M., the Bund Deutscher Mädel, *I* get chosen for Faith and Beauty too. Well, Inge, you know I don't spend lots of time in front of mirrors, and I don't think that much about my looks. But when she said that, I felt so flattered, my whole head started buzzing.

Meantime, my belly was aching too, but not worse than it had been off and on all week, and I ignored it.

"It's a good thing you moved to the Reich," Irmgard said, and started telling me about new things happening, like for instance huge modern sports arenas being built and *Autobahns* to everywhere and that no one goes hungry anymore, everybody has jobs, and most people own a Volkswagen and can go on vacations and have Strength Through Joy. And the terrific thing, she said, was that we, youth, to whom no one paid attention in the old days, are the most important part of it all. "Doesn't that make you proud, Lieselotte? Don't you thank your stars that you live here now?"

And, Inge, though you might not like me anymore, before I knew it, I'd answered, "Yes!"

"Of course you do!" She clapped me on the back. Then she reached forward, tapped Edeltraut on the shoulder, and said something into her ear.

Now Edeltraut turned around. She bit her lips together and without a word did what Irmgard had ordered her: She stuck the flag into my hands.

It's bloodred, with a white circle in the middle with a big black swastika. Inge, if you had seen me holding it, would you ever want to see me again? I didn't think about that then, I didn't think about anything. Now I can't think about anything else.

Irmgard said because this was my first Jungmädel hike, I should carry the flag for a while.

It puffed itself out before me in billows, from the wind. But I felt so strange, I felt as if my own breath from my lungs were rushing into it, making it billow like that, and as if it, the flag, were pulling me, instead of me carrying it. . . . Does that sound crazy to you? Can you possibly know what I mean?

Behind me everyone had started singing, "Our banner hurls us forward, on!/ Into the future march we, man for man." I sang too, the other voices seemed part of my voice, and mine of theirs: "We are marching for Hitler through night and through

need,/ With the banner for youth and for freedom,
for bread."

Holy Maria and Joseph, something's dripping
out of me, I suddenly thought in the middle of that,
I've wet my pants! But I can't have, the last time I
did that was when I was two! Then why do my
underpants feel wet? God, God, I prayed, please
don't let it run down my legs! I thought I'd die if
anybody saw. . . .

"Wasn't that inspiring," said Irmgard about the
singing. "Lieselotte, what's the matter? You're white
as a ghost! Are you sick?"

"I don't know—"

She grabbed the flag.

I ran into the woods as fast as one can with one's
thighs squeezed together. About twenty meters up
from the path there was a big rock, thank God, and
a clump of pines behind it. I crouched down back
there, and I pulled down my underpants. They're
grayish white, from having been washed a hundred
times. The crotch was bright, bright red. I was so
beside myself, for about a second I just stared down,
admiring the color, as if it were tulips or something
like that. Then I realized, That's blood, mine! And I
felt burning hot, even though it was pretty cold with
my underpants down, and I thought, I've hurt
myself, I don't know how, I don't know where, but
somewhere deep, too deep to ever heal. . . . Inge, can

you imagine? I could never tell this to anyone else as long as I live.

Of course, in about another second I started thinking like a normal person again. How could I have been so dumb?

Remember, when we made that bet, you said I was more "developed" than you, so I'd get my period first? Well, I got it, that was all.

I remembered I had toilet paper in my rucksack, I always bring some on hikes. I took it out and wiped myself. But even as I wiped, more blood came out of me. So then I made a wad of all the paper and stuck it between my legs and pulled my underpants up. But I doubted the paper would stay in place. And of course it slipped as soon as I moved. What was I going to do?

"Lieselotte," I heard Irmgard calling, "are you all right?" She'd come after me, but only as far as the rock. I thought that was very tactful of her.

"Yes," I called back. But my voice was shaking.

"Here, do you need this?" She handed me something over the rock. A towel, I thought. Then I saw it was a thick white pad stuffed with cotton, like the ones my mother makes out of old sheets and keeps in the bottom drawer of her sewing bureau. "Don't worry, Lieselotte, just think, it happens to half the people in the whole world, every single month," said Irmgard with a big smile. "Do you have any safety pins?"

I didn't. So she handed me two. "All right, now, all you do is pin the pad to your garter belt, front and back. Can you manage?"

I did. It felt warm and comforting and didn't slip when I came out from my hiding place.

"Welcome to womanhood!" Irmgard shook my hand. She gave me two more pads for later.

I was so grateful, I could have kissed her. "Thanks, Irmgard! You've been wonderful!"

"It's all in a Jungmädel leader's day's work. Come on, let's go back to the others."

We started walking to the path, hand in hand. And she asked me, "Is there anything you'd like to ask me?"

I knew she meant about periods and all that. But I felt as though I could confide in her about anything. So I asked, "Irmgard, do you believe the things people say about Jews?"

"Sure! Don't you?" She swung my hand back and forth and started singing cheerfully, "When Jewish blood spurts from our knives—"

Listen, Jungmädel girls don't carry knives as part of their equipment. But Hitler Youth boys do, even little ones who are only *Pimpfe,* like Rudi! And they're sharp, they're not toys!

Run, Lieselotte, run like a hare! Hide where the woods are thickest, live on berries and herbs, like in fairy tales, don't only think it, do it, I thought.

But in fairy tales it's usually summer, not November, and there aren't any berries now, and not a lot of herbs either. Besides, Irmgard can run too, I wouldn't have gotten far.

I took my hand out of hers and lagged behind a little, that was all.

Inge, you know that superstition, that people who're about to die see their whole past go by before their eyes?

Well, the opposite happened to me: Looking down at the path, seeing all those dark-skirted, wind-jacketed, brown-capped girls marching by, was like seeing my whole future. I'll have to march with them, do everything they make you do; there's no way out. It made me want to die. In my religion that's an awful sin. And I can't confess it. I happen to know that the priest I usually get has a brother who's Heinz's Hitler Youth leader. Oh, I know, priests don't betray things told to them in confession. Even so, I couldn't.

I just have to hope God can forgive me directly, without any absolution. And that God helps me stay as I am. Do you know what I mean? On the outside I will be like them, from the angle of my cap to how I tie my shoelaces. (They check up on all those things at inspection and give demerits. Demerits go down on your official Youth Movement record, which is more important than your school records and follows you for your whole life!) On the inside, God willing, I'll stay the me you know.

It's your turn to write. I'll save this till you do.

B.S.L.

Lieselotte

Thursday, November 11, 1937

Inge—

You know that song "The post it brings no mail for me?" Well, it didn't bring me any. Have you written to me yet? If not, hurry up and write! Oh, Inge, you don't know how lonely I feel!

Remember last spring when Susi König got her period and told almost our whole class, and how much we envied her? Well, there is not one girl in my whole class here to whom I'd even dream of telling such a thing.

Not having anyone to tell it to makes it seem less special. Soaking the blood out of the pads is a nuisance. Mutterl gave me an elastic belt to use instead of my garter belt. I don't have cramps anymore. I just hope a pin doesn't come undone and stick me in the belly right when I'm doing calisthenics or at some other embarrassing moment.

Of course I knew how Mutterl would be about it. Still, it was a letdown yesterday when I told her, all excited, and all she said was, "Shh, Lieselotte, not so loud!" As if the only thing that mattered was that such "women's business" shouldn't fall on Heinz's or Papa's manly ears. I think she was relieved I didn't need her to explain anything or show me what to do. She did show me where she keeps the pads, but I already knew that. And she said, "Don't take a bath." Baths are supposed to make you have worse cramps or something. But I really needed one after that hike. So I took one, and I felt fine.

I bet your mother will act different. If I ever have a daughter, I'll have a celebration for her when she gets her period.

I'm saving all these letters up to send you after you write to me, so hurry up already.

B.S.L.

Lieselotte

Friday, November 12, 1937

Dear Inge,

There's a catch to getting exempt from Religious Instruction. I would have known sooner if I had read the fine print on that form. You have to take National Socialist Ideology instead.

Heinz is taking it, of course. In his school they have it on Thursdays. It's about the force of history and the invisible bonds that unite all

Germans through Hitler and the destiny of the Aryan race—stuff which I already have up to here.

This morning after flag-raising and calisthenics Fräulein Schmidt called me up to her desk. "Lieselotte, you have still not handed in your Religious Instruction waiver form."

I had it right in my schoolbag, with Papa's signature on it. "I know, Fräulein Schmidt."

"Why not? Didn't your mother or father want to sign it?"

"Um, no, I mean, yes, that's why not."

"Tsk, tsk, that is a shame. You see, our school is hoping to win a special citation for high enrollment in National Socialist Ideology. Would it help if I spoke to your parents?"

"Oh, no, thank you, Fräulein Schmidt. I really don't think it would help."

"Well, you'll just have to go to Religious Instruction, then." And I did, with only three other girls from my class. All the rest take National Socialist Ideology.

The priest is Father Andreas. He teaches it by the semolina-pudding method, asking the same old questions, hearing the same old answers rattled off.

Wouldn't you know, the question he asked me was, "What are we commanded to do by the Eighth

Commandment?" The answer is, To speak with truth, etc. Well, I hadn't, exactly, to Fräulein Schmidt a while ago. But I didn't feel too ashamed. The untruth I told is so harmless, it couldn't hurt a flea!

At the end of the lesson Father Andreas gave out saints' pictures. I got one of St. Francis with animals around him, a white-tailed deer, a fawn, some big-eared hares, a blue bird on his shoulder, and a green bird in the distance, though it looked as though it was sitting on his halo.

"Oh, yours is so pretty! Please, please trade!" said the girl next to me. I took one look at hers, a miserable-looking saint with a twisted face as if she'd just had all her teeth pulled out, and I said, "No, thanks." But then I looked again and noticed her wreath of roses and recognized her—Santa Rosalia. That's my mother's patron saint. So I said, "All right."

I gave the picture to Mutterl. So then she realized I'd gone to Religious Instruction after all, and she was as happy as on her name day, when we brought her flowers and breakfast in bed. It was a big worry off her mind. "But don't tell Papa," she said.

I used to think that married couples told each other everything. Do your parents?

B.S.L.

Lieselotte

Saturday, November 13, 1937

Inge—

Listen, I'm starting to hate the postman with his shiny buttons and smile from ear to ear. Of course it's not his fault. How long will I still have to wait?

Last night at supper Papa said, "Well, Lieselotte, what did they teach you in National Socialist Ideology today?"

"Does anyone want more meat?" Mutterl asked, to give me time to make up something.

"Well, let's see. We learned about Faith, and Beauty. And, Papa, you know what my teacher thinks? Someday I might get picked for it."

"You?" Heinz let out a snort. "With those pimples you're sprouting? And that horse's tail?"

Papa told him to shut up, for once. He reached across the table and shook my hand. "That would make me really proud, Lieselotte."

I suppose I could have made up something not so conceited-sounding. But as untruths go, I don't suppose this one will hurt a flea either.

Now I'll go take a bath and get dressed for the folk dance. At least we don't have to wear uniforms. I'm wearing my winter dirndl with the rose-colored bodice and silver buttons shaped like rosebuds. If only the boys at it weren't all in the Hitler Youth!

But that's like wishing the man in the moon were going to be there.

When are you going to write to me?

B.S.L.

Lieselotte

Tuesday, November 16, 1937
Written in a broom closet in Scholz-Klink

Inge—

Finally your letter came! Thank you a thousand million times! Only, why, why, why did you address it care of Scholz-Klink?

This broom closet, with a naked lightbulb hanging down, and just big enough to sit down in, is the only place in this whole big school with any privacy, so I ducked into here and I read it.

What did you do with my home address? Eat it for breakfast with butter and jam? Stick it in your coal-stove? Wipe your pen with it?

The janitor may need his broom any moment. I think I hear his footsteps. Anyway, I have to leave this lovely hideaway or I'll be late for Housewifely Arts and will be in still more trouble—if such a thing is possible. Wait till I tell you!

During Recess
Luckily it's raining out, so they're letting us stay in

homeroom and we can use recess as a study period if we need to. I need to! I'm writing this in my German composition notebook in case anyone gets nosy. By "anyone" you know whom I mean. E.W. are her initials, my neighbor and dutiful watchdog. How much nicer a dog would be! But I'm wasting time. Listen, this morning, into this same homeroom, right after calisthenics, came Fräulein Pfitzner, and crooked her finger at me. "Lieselotte Vessely?"

"Yes?"

"Come with me. Frau Direktor Seidlmeier wishes to see you." She wouldn't tell me what about.

She led me down the corridor. I looked into the faces of the people on the posters on the walls: tanned young Labor Service men and women, harvesting wheat in sunny fields; families on vacations; workmen with bulging arm muscles, raising their fists, saying, "Germany, awake!" I wondered whether any of them ever had to go to their Herr or Frau Direktor's office when they were in school. And if so, whether they'd had as much dread in their hearts as I had in mine. I doubted it. They all looked so proud and so pleased with themselves.

Fräulein Pfitzner showed me in to Frau Direktor Seidlmeier's office.

"*Heil Hitler*, Lieselotte," said Frau Direktor Seidlmeier—with your letter in her hand!

"That's for me!" I reached for it.

"Sit down, Lieselotte." She held it up in front of me, close enough so I could read your writing on the envelope. "Have you any idea why you would be the recipient of a letter addressed in this unusual way?"

"No, Frau Direktor. But I've been waiting for it a long time. Please, may I have it?"

She sat down at her desk. She took a letter opener and slit the envelope open. It made a tearing noise, as if it were screaming.

"Ahem," and she started reading, "'Dear Lieselotte, It seems like a year—'"

"No, please, Frau Direktor!" I couldn't bear to hear *your* words in *her* voice.

She looked as surprised as if the desk or chair had talked back to her. "Very well, if you prefer, I'll read it to myself."

She took her time. It felt like a century.

Finally she put the letter down in her lap. I know this sounds crazy, but I thought it looked like a little animal's, a squirrel's, underbelly, white and helpless against her dark brown skirt; or like a little patch of snow that could melt away. I worried that she'd end up not giving it to me.

"Well, Lieselotte, I won't embarrass you by asking who Herr Professor Hedgehog is supposed to be or what Edeltraut Wiecks has done to deserve a kick. But be so kind as to tell me, what is B.S.L.?"

Inge, remember, in *Beneath Distant Skies* when the Comanches tied Swift Eagle to the stake and the chief asked him questions and he didn't answer? Well, I said, "Please, Frau Direktor, don't think I'm being impertinent, but it's something very personal."

"All right, never mind, you're just children, keep your secret."

I thought that was nice of her.

Then she said, "Your friend Inge Dornenwald is Jewish, am I right? That's why she sent the letter here—so your parents won't know that she's writing to you. To go behind your parents' backs!"

"Oh, no, Frau Direktor, it's nothing like that! She must have just lost my address or something."

"Or something," said Frau Direktor Seidlmeier sarcastically. She pulled the telephone near to her. "What is your number at home?"

I gave it.

She dialed it.

I prayed, Holy Mother of God, let Mutterl answer. She will, she will, I assured myself. Papa's not home at this hour. He's at his office or out at the barracks of the Austrian Legion, where he also sometimes works. In any case, I offered to make a novena if Mutterl picked up the telephone. Well, I won't have to make a novena.

"Hello, Herr Vessely? This is Frau Direktor Seidlmeier of Scholz-Klink speaking." And she told him about your letter coming to me in care of the school.

He said something.

"You did? I see. Well, that explains it," said Frau Direktor Seidlmeier, and she nodded understandingly.

My father said something else.

"Well, I think that Lieselotte would adjust faster if you changed your mind and gave permission for her to take our fine course in National Socialist Ideolo—"

"Sapperlot!" I heard my father yell into the telephone. "I *gave* permission! I signed that form a week ago!"

"Did you? Be so kind as to hold the wire a moment." Frau Direktor Seidlmeier turned her ice-gray eyes on me. "Lieselotte, may I ask, where is the waiver form your father signed?"

Her stare was like two icicles boring holes into me. I took the waiver form out of my schoolbag and handed it to her.

"Hello, Herr Vessely? I have cleared the matter up. I have the form now, yes."

He said something.

"That, of course, is entirely up to you, Herr Vessely. I'm glad we had this little talk. *Heil Hitler.*" Frau Direktor Seidlmeier hung up.

She turned to me. She told me I'd failed in my chief daughterly duty, namely, obeying my father.

She did not want to hear my reasons, no. She hoped, however, that I would take her advice. The first part of it was that I should be sure to appear in National Socialist Ideology next Friday and make up for what I'd missed by doing extra work. The second part of her advice was not to write to you.

She isn't punishing me. She guesses my father will take care of that.

"Can I have my letter now, please, Frau Direktor?"

She gave it to me, finally. "You may go now, Lieselotte."

So I rushed into that broom closet and read it, at last. And I wished there were a trapdoor in the floor to a secret passageway, I wouldn't care how long and winding, dank and dark, even a few rats running by would be all right with me if only it led to another trapdoor in the floor of a janitor's broom closet in good old Herrengasse Gymnasium. . . .

I don't know if you can imagine how much I dread going home for noon meal. You don't know what my father's like. Well, I'll tell you: His favorite curse is *Sapperlot*. His favorite song is "At the White Horse Inn on Wolfgang See." His favorite dish is roast leg of veal. He likes dark beer better than light, and when he wants to tease my mother, he says any beer tastes better in the beer hall than at home. He used to smoke a pipe, but when we moved here, he switched to cigarettes because there are different photographs of Hitler in every pack and Heinz collects them. He has his hair cut shorter now. He looks handsome in his uniform. But all that is on the outside. What's he like on the inside? To tell you the truth, I really don't know. I don't know him that well. Heinz knows him much better. Heinz is closer to him, they have man-boy things in common. Do you know what I mean? If you don't, it's because you have both your parents all to yourself. All I know is, I hope he's eating noon meal out somewhere today. . . .

Still Tuesday, November 16, 1937

Dear Inge,

If my handwriting looks shaky, it's because my hand is shaking. So is all of me.

When I came home for noon meal, my father stood at the top of the stairs, waiting for me. He said, "Take your coat off. Go in the living room."

I went in there.

"Lean over that chair."

My father took his belt off. It made a hum in the air and came down across my back.

I screamed. I sounded like an animal.

"That one was for 'Faith'!" my father said.

Again.

"That one was for 'Beauty.'"

One more time. "And that one was for lying to me. There, I'm through. Stop screaming or the Pfaltzes will think we're roasting you on a spit."

I stayed bent over the chair. I retched till I threw up. When I was done, I felt rid of any good feeling I'd ever had for him.

Mutterl came in. She'd been standing in the kitchen, holding her ears and crying. She was still crying. She cleaned up the mess.

Inge, this is the last letter I will write you. And I can't ever send it. Or the others either.

I know now why you wrote to me c/o Scholz-Klink. My father told me: He took my letter from the little shelf in the hall where we always put mail for the postman to pick up, and he crossed out the return address so you wouldn't be able to write me back. He figured that way I wouldn't write to you anymore, and we'd just naturally forget each other. Then he put my letter back on the shelf so you'd get it. He thinks that was very soft-hearted of him.

Listen, he has a colleague in the SA, a Herr Griesshof, whose wife was writing letters to someone Herr Griesshof didn't like. So he asked some people he knew in the SD to be on the lookout for the letters. The SD is the Security Department. It's huge. One out of every ten Germans works for it, in secret. There are SD people everywhere—in factories, in schools, in offices, and of course in post offices. Well, Herr Griesshof soon got hold of Frau Griesshof's letters. Now there is a new Frau Griesshof. The old one is in jail. So is the person to whom she was writing.

My father is about to be promoted to the rank of *Obersturmführer*. And he says that the daughter of an SA *Obersturmführer* should not be corresponding with a Jewess.

He made me swear I wouldn't anymore.

He said that when the Anschluss comes, many Austrians living here will move back to Austria, and we will be among them. At least he, Mutterl, and Heinz will. If I break my word to him, he will leave me behind with his sister, Aunt Louisa. He has already asked her if she would take me, and she said yes.

Inge, I once had a cowbell that a peasant woman who lived near my grandparents' farm gave to me when I was little, a long time ago, when I didn't know you yet. It sounded like green meadows and cows coming back to their barn after grazing on clover all day. I rang it and rang it. Then Heinz wanted to ring it, and he grabbed it. I grabbed it back, and the clapper came out. So then it was mute. I stuck it away somewhere. I don't have it anymore.

I feel like that bell now.

What good does it do to send B.S.L. and sign this,

Your Lieselotte?

Vienna, March 15, 1938

P.S. Now you understand.

Excuse the scrawl, I have to write fast, Mitzi is in a hurry.

Inge, I'm sorry you couldn't come this morning, I wanted to see you!

Tomorrow I think "the coast will be clear." So meet me at the Embankment at ten o'clock. If you can't, let "Anni H." call me up. The number is 17-0-19.

If I can't, "Anni" will call you.

Four

I woke up with the greatest feeling—of everything that's been wrong now being right. I rubbed my eyes, I had to think: But Hitler's here, the Anschluss is happening, Herr Plattau's dead, already buried—oh, but Lieselotte's letters! They were what the feeling was about. Whatever else changed, her friendship did not!

And no call came from "Anni Hopf" to spoil our plans. At nine thirty I got ready to go.

"Where are you off to so cheerfully?" Mutti asked.

"O.O. wants me to see where he's worked all these years." That was true. Today was his last day at the office, and I had told him I'd meet him there—at noon.

I headed for the Stadtpark.

Lieselotte and Schnackerl were already down at the Embankment. Schnackerl greeted me as though he remembered me from the day before yesterday. Of course he does, says Lieselotte.

I said, "Thank you for the letters. I read them so many times, I know them by heart almost."

"Good, I'm glad."

I asked how come the coast was so clear today.

Because her father was out in Hüttelsdorf, "repatriating" some Austrian Legion soldiers (that's part of his job); and Heinz was at a Hitler Youth Leadership training session in Hietzing; and Frau Vessely—not that she'd mind our meeting each other—was helping at Uncle Ludwig's because his housekeeper (the one I thought looked like a witch) has a bad case of lumbago.

Meanwhile Schnackerl frisked around in the bushes. Lieselotte had let him off the leash. "Come back here!" she called. "You know, he's actually Schnackerl the Second."

He came running.

"Want to hear about Schnackerl the First?"

I said, "Yes."

So then we walked all along the Embankment to where the Wien disappears into an underground tunnel, and she told me this story:

A week before Christmas she and the children from downstairs, Rudi and Uta Pfaltz, were in the garden. It had snowed. They were building a snowman.

Heinz and a boy from his class, Werner, burst in through the gate. Two others, Toni and Uli, climbed over the fence. They were all in uniform, they had a Hitler Youth meeting later that afternoon.

Werner shouted, "*Heh*, Lieselotte, look what we brought!"

Heinz held something in his arms. The others crowded around him, so at first Lieselotte couldn't see. Then Heinz set it down in the snow. It was a dachshund puppy, the color of chestnuts.

"Isn't that Schnackerl?" said Uta. "What's he doing here?"

"He's peeing on our snowman! Stop it, naughty dog!" Rudi yelled.

Werner grabbed the puppy up and gave him a smack on the snout.

The puppy whined.

"Hic, hic," went the others, "we have *Schnackerl*" (that's slang for hiccups) "hic, hic, hic, ha ha!"

"But Schnackerl is the Weintraubs' dog," said Rudi.

"Not anymore. We rescued him," said Heinz, while Schnackerl squirmed in Werner's arms.

"From what?" asked Lieselotte.

"From racial shame. The Weintraubs are Jews, and Jews aren't supposed to mingle with Aryans. Give him here, Werner." Heinz took Schnackerl and looked between his hind legs. "*Jawohl,* just as I thought: not circumcised! That proves it, he's an Aryan dog!"

Werner, Toni, and Uli laughed like mad.

"What's circumcised?" asked Uta.

"It's a line around your wee-wee maker," Rudi said.

Uta giggled.

"Very funny. Dogs don't get circumcised! Put him down, he hates how you're holding him," said Lieselotte.

"Here, Uli!" Heinz passed him to Uli like a soccer ball. Uli passed him to Toni, and Toni, to Werner. "Hurray for the Aryan dog, the dog of pure and noble blood," they yelled.

"Wait a minute," Werner said. "'Schnackerl' isn't such a noble name."

"True," said Toni. "Let's baptize him something else."

"Let's!" Heinz picked up some snow.

"Don't you dare!" Lieselotte knocked the snow out of Heinz's hands.

He grabbed up some more and threw it at her. "You're right,

we should baptize him properly. Rudi, go inside and bring us out some water."

"Rudi, don't," said Lieselotte. But he was already going to the door.

Werner pulled the puppy's paw. "*Heh,* look at Schnackerl saluting!"

Schnackerl barked and snapped.

"Don't tease him like that! Let me have him." Lieselotte tried to take him from Werner. But Uta pulled at her sleeve. "Lieselotte, I have to go to the toilet! I can't undo my leggings by myself."

Lieselotte had to go with her. At the door they met Rudi coming out with a jug of water. "Spill that on the ground or I'll never take care of you again!" said Lieselotte.

But Rudi gave the water to the boys.

When Lieselotte and Uta came back out, the "baptism" was done. Schnackerl shivered. He looked half-drowned.

"Let's name him Ulrich," said Uli.

"No, Dackl von Hunding," said Werner.

"No, let's name him Heinrich, after Heinz, because it was Heinz's idea to rescue him," said Toni, and the others agreed.

Heinz was thrilled. "*Heh,* thanks, that's decent of you! Now he's my god-dog! Werner, let him get down. All right, Heinrich my god-dog, now run around."

The puppy still shivered. And he peed all over the place.

"*Heh,* it's a quarter past four already, we'll be late to the meeting," said Werner.

Heinz wanted to take "Heinrich." But the others said no, the den leader wouldn't like it.

So Heinz told Lieselotte, "You take care of him. Don't let him out of your sight. If he's not here when I get back, I'll beat you up." And he and the others left.

Lieselotte sat down with Schnackerl and held him quietly till he relaxed. Then she let Uta and Rudi play with him.

Soon Frau Pfaltz came home and took the children inside. By then Schnackerl was worn out and went to sleep, in Lieselotte's lap. When he woke up, she looked on his dog license for the Weintraubs' address. They lived nearby, and she took him home.

When Heinz came back from the meeting, just as he'd promised, he beat her up. She gave him back a few punches, and they stayed angry with each other. "At least I stayed angry with him," Lieselotte said. "For the first time since I can remember, I didn't give him anything for Christmas."

"Good, serves him right. Do you know what he did to me?" I told her about seeing him outside the skating rink on that Sunday, our birthday. "That was Heinz, wasn't it?"

"Yes. He and Papa came here that weekend. You can imagine how much *I* wanted to! But listen, for Christmas he went with Papa to at least six or seven pet stores. He kept saying, 'No, not this one, not that one,' till finally they found a puppy who looked exactly like Schnackerl. And he chipped in his allowance from I don't know how many weeks, and they bought him for me. That's why I sent you that postcard, to show you what I got! So it didn't serve Heinz that right, me not giving him anything—do you see?"

"Yes." I saw. You can have a brother who does awful things

and is awful, is a Nazi, but that doesn't mean he doesn't love you. It's complicated. I didn't know what to say about it. I asked, "Did you see Schnackerl the First after that? Did the two ever meet?"

"No. I think the Weintraubs moved away around then. Speaking of that—are *you* going to?"

"Yes, we don't know where to or when yet. But listen, you've only just come back, so let's not talk about moving away, all right? Anyway, I'm sure we won't till after Mitzi's wedding. She's so happy! She and Fredl already made up." And we talked about the wedding and my bridesmaid's dress and what Lieselotte will wear, because of course she's invited too.

Then it was almost noon and I had to go to meet O.O.

"Same time, same place tomorrow, Lieselotte?"

"Naturally, if there is still no school and the coast is clear."

O.O. showed me around the Eldorado offices, introduced me to colleagues, and finished saying his good-byes.

Then we went to a travel bureau, and he bought himself a ticket for America on the huge steamship *Regina d'Italia*. They gave us a brochure of it. It looks as long as from our house to the Löwengasse. It has three smokestacks; also, ballrooms, shops, and a swimming pool, only the weather will be too cold for swimming. It sails next Monday, from Genoa. Mutti walks well enough already, so O.O.'s not worried about that anymore; as for our quota numbers, we'll surely have them by then.

Vati went to the consulate yesterday after he got home from the funeral, but it was still closed on account of the Anschluss. He went again this morning, very early. I hope the line wasn't too long.

After the travel bureau O.O. and I went to a wine store, and O.O. bought a bottle of very good champagne, just in case.

Later

The champagne stayed in the icebox. The line in front of the consulate was so long, Vati waited almost the whole day, but he didn't get inside.

Thursday, March 17

A notice came from school: It won't reopen till next Monday. Lieselotte's coast wasn't clear today. So I stayed home and helped Mutti. She has been spending lots of time writing letters to friends, relatives, and acquaintances abroad, even very distant ones, even ones we hardly know, asking whether they can help us get visas. That has put her behind in her work for Huber Verlag, and Gustl, the messenger, was due. So I checked a stack of manuscripts, making sure they were complete.

Gustl came an hour early.

"Go in the kitchen, have your coffee as usual. By the time you're finished, I'll be done," Mutti said.

He shuffled his feet and said he couldn't wait.

"Where's the work for next week?" I asked.

"Don't ask me, I'm just the messenger." He took the stack of manuscripts. "Well, *Heil Hit*—I mean, *Grüss Gott*, Frau Dornenwald."

Mutti said, "It's not your fault," and wished him luck for the future. "*Leh wohl*, Gustl." You only say *Leh wohl* to someone you don't expect to see again.

"That's not fair! They can't do that to you!" I shouted when Gustl had gone.

Then Herr Huber called up. Polite as she'd been to Gustl, now she yelled into the telephone, because it was Herr Huber's fault. I could hear her from the living room: "Don't give me those excuses. I've worked for you for so many years, you can tell it to me straight. You're firing your Jewish employees." She didn't say *Leh wohl*. She banged the telephone down.

I was glad she let go like that.

"Oh, well, what's fourteen years?" she said, coming out of the study. She leaned on me and went back to bed. I thought how I'd feel if I just got one bad mark on schoolwork I'd done well. I said, "Fourteen years is a whole long career. It's terrible what they're doing."

"The swine! Kurt Huber too. Oh, poor old Kurt." She mimicked his voice: "'Hanne, try to understand, I have no choice, it's not my idea, it's official policy, I have no choice, I'm merely following the directive.' *Pfui!* There, so ends my outburst."

I said, "Mutti, don't feel so bad. *They* should feel bad, they won't find anyone as good as you. But you'll get another job, maybe a better one, wherever we go."

She shook her head. "Jobs like that don't grow on trees. Besides, one has to know the language. Don't worry, though, I'm keeping my perspective. The important thing is to get out, safe and soon. If only your father gets those quota numbers today!"

While we were on the subject I said, "I've never understood what quota numbers are."

So she explained: America is one of the few places that lets in lots of people from other countries. The way it does this is by the quota system, which means a certain number of people from every country are allowed in every year, say, for instance, eight thousand a year from Austria. That eight thousand is Austria's quota. And every person who wants to go, gets a number and has to wait till it's that number's turn.

"If so many people want to go, won't it still be a very long wait, even after we have the numbers?" I asked.

"Yes. But it gives us a better chance to get temporary visas to other countries, say, for instance, Switzerland or Czechoslovakia."

"Or Yugoslavia?"

"Yes, I suppose. You see, those countries mind less letting refugees in if they know those refugees won't stay indefinitely but are going to America."

"Why?"

"Oh, because those countries are overcrowded and have economic problems, and because the world just isn't a very hospitable place."

Later

It's complicated, but understanding it made me appreciate it more when Vati burst in tonight happy, swinging his briefcase, saying, "Well, it took all day, but I got them!"

"Our quota numbers! Oh, Franzl!" Mutti hobbled to him. "I'm especially glad because I hear there are many publishing firms in America, much better ones than measly old Huber Verlag."

So now Vati knew. "You mean they fired you, those dirty dogs?"

It was such a childish name, they both laughed, and Vati took her in his arms.

After supper O.O. brought out the champagne. We invited Mitzi in, and we celebrated.

O.O. was toastmaster.

The first toast was to Mutti's hip for starting to mend so well. O.O. and she, with just one crutch, did a waltz, slow and clumpy, around the room, to the tune of O.O. humming the Emperor Waltz.

Then O.O. poured everyone another little sip, and we drank to the Liberty Statue, which is in the harbor of New York. O.O. said he will meet us there whenever our boat arrives.

Champagne is the best wine there is. It has fizz, like soda, only finer, and it makes you feel better with every swallow even if there were certain things you started out feeling bad about.

Next we drank a toast to Mitzi and Fredl's happiness. O.O. said, "Inge, sing the 'Wedding March' from *Lohengrin*." Ordinarily I would have been embarrassed. But with so many sips of champagne in me, I sang it quite loudly.

That must have been when the doorbell rang and nobody heard it.

Vati and Mitzi had just linked arms and were clinking glasses when suddenly a tall figure in a muskrat fur appeared, as if out of nowhere. It was Usch. The room felt suddenly different. Maybe she let in a cold draft. In any case I shivered.

She carried a black leather briefcase. She said, "Good evening, all. I rang the bell, but nobody came. So I took the liberty of letting myself in." (She'd used the extra key Oma Sofie has to our apartment.) "I hope I'm not disturbing you."

"Of course not," Vati said. "You're just in time to drink a toast with us."

"Let me pour you a drop of champagne," said O.O.

"Thank you, no, I never drink. Frau Dornenwald wished me to bring this briefcase over. She was afraid it might be forgotten in the confusion of packing."

Oma Sofie is leaving on Saturday, for Switzerland.

Usch handed the briefcase to my father. "Here, Franzi," she started to say. She often still calls him that. But she corrected herself and called him "Herr Dornenwald."

The briefcase was full of his old schoolwork, report cards, diplomas, and things like that. It also had his discharge papers from the army after the World War.

"Frau Dornenwald also wanted me to ask whether she by any chance left her pillbox here. The little round one with the mother-of-pearl inlaid lid."

"I don't think so," Vati said.

"Mitzi, perhaps you found it while cleaning?" Usch asked.

"No."

Usch gave Mitzi a look that said, Then you can't have cleaned very hard.

Mitzi handed me her champagne glass to hold. She ducked down and looked under the bed. "No pillbox down there. Perhaps you'd like to look for yourself," she invited Usch. "That way you can check if it's dusty down there."

"No need to be impertinent, my girl," Usch whispered. To us she said, "Again, beg pardon for disturbing. Good night, everyone."

Vati saw her out.

Friday, March 18

This morning I met Lieselotte for a little while in front of the Urania. I saw her coming, but I didn't recognize her. She was in her uniform. I know, I know, she has to belong to Jungmädel, but it was still a shock. I guess it showed in my face, because she said, "I'm not exactly wild about this outfit either."

"I know. I shouldn't have looked like that."

Across from the Urania is a little park with benches. We sat there for fifteen minutes. Then she had to go—to Jungmädel headquarters. She had made a bargain with her father: She'd fold leaflets there today. In return, he'd let her go to Uncle Ludwig's on Sunday. Uncle Ludwig is having some sort of reception.

"I have an idea," said Lieselotte. "Why don't you come to it? It'll be fun. Mutterl is baking things for it. Uncle Ludwig will be glad to see you again. Mutterl too. She said so. Can you, Inge?"

"I'd love to! I'm sure I can. Oh, wait a minute—what time will it be?"

"Three o'clock."

"No. That's when O.O.'s train leaves for Genoa, and I'm going to see him off." I wouldn't miss that for anything.

"Then when can we see each other?"

"Not tomorrow either. Oma Sofie leaves for Switzerland. I'm seeing her off too. And Monday's school." We arranged to meet in the little courtyard off the Schwedenplatz at twenty after eight on Monday so at least we could walk from there together.

When I got back to our house, I met Evi on the stairs. She asked, "How come you didn't come up yesterday? You said you would."

I'd forgotten. "Oh, Evi, I'm sorry!"

"Oh, that's all right. Inge, you know what just happened to me?" She had been to Wegner's to buy sugar for her mother. And Herr Wegner had waited on three customers first, even though they had come in after her.

I said, "I know, he does the same thing to me. He says we're lucky he sells us stuff at all."

"Because we're Jewish?" She's so innocent, she just can't believe it, even though it's happening right under her nose.

So I joked, "Of course not! Why would you think a thing like that? It's only because we dropped down from the moon. Herr Wegner doesn't like moon people. He's having a sign made up, Moon People Undesired on These Premises!"

At least it made her laugh. "Come upstairs with me now, all right? I have new paper dolls, of the Dionne Quintuplets!"

"Paper dolls? Oh, Evi, aren't you ever going to grow up? I can't come right now. I have to do something with my grandfather. I'll come in a little while."

"All right. But promise you won't forget."

I had to give O.O. his *th* practice. I do that every day. He is very eager to learn to make that sound by the time he gets to America. I say, "This, that, these, those, thanks, theater, thistle, thousand." I show him where I put my tongue: behind my upper teeth. Then he tries to put his tongue behind his upper teeth, he tries really hard. And he says, "Ziss, zat, zese, zose," etc.

Now I'll go to Evi's. I'm taking my necklace. I'll ask whether we can go to her father's store. Maybe he can fix it.

Later

I think Evi grew up about five years' worth in just one hour or so of today. I'll try to write about what happened like I did about when they took Vati and O.O. to clean streets on Saturday—very calmly, in an orderly way (Fräulein Pappenheim would approve). Or I won't be able to write about it at all.

Evi said, Sure, her father could easily fix my necklace. Frau Fried had just baked some plum buns. She gave us four, two to eat on the way, and two for Herr Fried. And we went.

His store is on the Praterstrasse, in the Second District, about a fifteen-minute walk.

When we were nearly there, a car drove by, and the sun hit the windshield in such a way, it made a glare that hurt my eyes. I put my hand over my eyes. When I took my hand away, I thought my eyes were not working right—because the glass window of Herr Fried's jewelry store looked all zigzagged to me. And inside the floor was covered with bright somethings that caught the sunlight and flashed.

"Papa, Papa!" Evi was screaming.

My eyes worked all right. The window was zigzagged, it was smashed! The things on the floor were jagged pieces of glass.

"Children, look out! Don't cut yourselves!" Herr Fried rushed to us, pulled Evi to him, put her head against his chest.

He is quite a stout man, his chest bulges out. His face was paper-white and sweating. But his voice did not shake. He said to me, "I'm glad you came to see my store. I only wish I could show it to you under better circumstances."

Everything smashable was smashed. Everything liftable— jewelry, watches, money—was stolen. The cash register drawers gaped open.

"Who did this?" I asked.

He shrugged. "SA men, SS men, what's the difference what initials? Six of them, no, seven. In any case, too many. So I went quietly into my workroom in the back, closed the door behind me, and prayed they shouldn't come after me and do to me what they did to the window and the display cases. Glass can be replaced. People, not."

"Did you call the police?" Evi asked.

"Evilein, no. One of them *was* a policeman."

"What are you going to do, Papa?"

"First I'm going to guess what's in that bag." He sniffed the air. "Mm, that's easy, plum buns. Next"—he reached into the bag—"I'll eat one."

"Papa, please, you don't have to act so cheerful just for me," said Evi.

"I know, my kitten. But I feel cheerful now that you are here.

Although I would rather have spared you having to see this with your own eyes."

He took us into his workroom. "See, in here, thank God, everything is still in order."

"Papa, Inge's necklace br—"

"Evi, shh, not now!" I didn't think she should bother him with that.

"Inge's necklace broke? Don't be shy, let me see."

So I gave it to him. He took a tiny pair of pliers, and he pinched the broken links together. He slipped the Mogen Dovid back on. "Allow me." He fastened it around my neck.

"Thank you very much, Herr Fried."

"Thank *you*. Now at least my day was not a total loss. Now you two should go home."

"Papa, you come with us," said Evi.

No, he had to wait for a glazier to come and tell him how much it will cost to fix everything.

"Then I'll stay too," said Evi.

I said, "I'd better go home." Then I stood there, trying to think what I could say that would be suitable and show how sorry I felt. Finally I came up with, "I'm so sorry," which is also suitable for when somebody has stubbed his toe.

Going home by myself, I had awful thoughts: Like, that the hole they smashed in Herr Fried's store window is connected to the hole in the world I thought I was just making up as a way of writing how I felt on Saturday, and so that hole is just as real. This doesn't sound as though it makes sense, but it does to me.

Then I thought of Herr Vessely and wondered whether he smashes windows in. And just then, across the street, I saw a bunch of people standing around outside a stationery store. A little boy with a skullcap on was painting JEW on the window. A man in leather pants with a swastika armband on was making him do it. I only saw it for a second. I didn't need to look longer than that. It will always be there in my mind, and so will Herr Fried's store, smashed in, even when I'm an old, old woman with more brown age spots on my hands than O.O. has.

Saturday, March 19

Oma Sofie was able to get a Swiss visa because Aunt Emmi and Uncle Hugo are her sponsors and signed a lot of declarations that they are able to support her and she will never be a burden on the state of Switzerland.

I asked Vati how come they can't sponsor us too. Because they are not that rich, Vati said. They couldn't support us too, and the government knows that and won't let them sponsor us.

Vati, Usch, and I saw Oma Sofie off.

The Westbahnhof was much more crowded than it is when we go to Mondsee from there. I saw many sad partings with kissing and crying and all that.

To be absolutely honest, I don't think I will miss Oma Sofie so much, and I didn't feel as sad as I will feel tomorrow.

On the streetcar back Usch put her head on my father's shoulder. "Some people can't help crying," she said, and cried some more. She had already cried plenty before at the station. I know she really loves Oma Sofie. But I couldn't help thinking these new tears were meant to show me up for not having cried at all. But then a long curved hairpin fell out of the knot she wears her hair in. She's so careful about that knot at the back of her neck, I never saw it undone. But now whole strands of her heavy brown-gray hair came loose and fell down over Vati's coat, and she didn't even notice. So I changed my mind. I decided she was crying because she couldn't help it, she was that sad. And for once in my life, though I didn't start liking her any better, I felt sorry for her.

"Oh, Franzi, I'll miss her so much," she moaned.

"Of course you will," said Vati. "I will too."

"But it's different for you. You have your family. I'm an old woman, I have nobody now."

"Usch, don't talk like that, you still have us," said Vati.

"But you'll be leaving. Then where will I be? Oh, Franzi, you can't know, but I was young once, I was not so bad-looking, quite a few young men asked me to marry them, but I turned them all down. Working for your parents, bringing you up and your brother and your sister, that was the only life I've had. Your parents' home was my only home since my girlhood." She buried her face in his coat.

He patted her on the back. "It's still your home, Usch. You know my mother has paid the rent through June."

"I know. That was so good of her. But after that, what will I do?" Usch sobbed on Vati's shoulder.

———

Sunday, March 20

Today is the day I've been dreading.

O.O. got up very early. So did I. I kept him company while he shaved. Not so much because I still enjoy watching people shave as to spend every moment I could with him.

His eyes had their droopy look. His cheeks and chin were white with lather. He resembled a St. Bernard more than ever.

He said, "Let me practice *th*'s one more time. See, I put my tongue where you told me, and I say it: Zzz! Zanks. Zousands. Not good?"

"No, but never mind. If people from America had to pronounce Viennese sounds, they wouldn't get them right either, for a long time. O.O., do you think you'll be homesick?"

"I'll be homesick for people, yes. But not for Vienna. Any place that wants to be 'Jew-cleansed' is no home of mine."

"What time is your train to Genoa?"

"At ten past three. Why? You are not coming along to the station."

I thought he was joking. "Of course I am!"

"No, Inge. You went yesterday. Wasn't that enough?"

"But O.O., this is different, I want to!"

"On the day I leave, what counts is what *I* want. And I want you not to."

"Why not?"

"Because I have it all figured out where you should go: to the Wurstelprater." He put on a clownish smile, dabbed shaving lather on his nose, and said, "Inge, please, for me. It will give me pleasure when I'm sitting in the train to think of you eating a

Würstel, drinking a *Kracherl,* and going on the Giant Ferris Wheel, seeing the whole city spread out below."

He is going to be homesick, no matter how he denies it, I was thinking. But then he said, "Most of all I want you to give the *Watschenmann* a pair of smacks, good and hard, one on each cheek, from me, as my special farewell to Vienna, with all your might so the strength measure will zoom way up and ring the bell, *clang, clang!*"

When he finished shaving, he gave me ten schillings.

"O.O., that's much too much!"

"Not if you go on all the rides. And take Mitzi along. Maybe Fredl too. After all, I don't expect you to go to the Wurstelprater alone."

Then he and I had our farewell, in private.

I told him, "By the way, O.O., the book you gave me for Chanukah is almost all filled up."

That pleased him. He said, "Stay clever and good. I'll see you in America."

"What if we don't get there?"

"You will. Now give me a kiss."

I gave him a kiss. His mustache doesn't bother me at all anymore. But one thing I don't like to do is tell people I love them, even when it's true. I always think that must embarrass people very much. It does me. So I said, "O.O., I'm really glad I've gotten to know you. You are someone very special in my life."

"And you, in mine."

Then he laid his hand on top of my head. He didn't say it out loud, but I knew he was blessing me.

Mutti has been practicing walking, but without overdoing it, and has been making such progress, Dr. Feuerwerker told her yesterday that she is ready to go out. So today she put on her most stylish suit, a plaid one, and a beige hat with a wide brim. I haven't seen her look so pretty in a long time. She only took one crutch, making hardly any noise with it. And she and Vati went with O.O. to the train.

It was the first time I'd seen her go out of the apartment door on her own two feet in almost six weeks.

Feel proud of her, I told myself, and I tried to. But I thought, *I'm* at least as close to O.O. as she is! And I felt cheated, jealous, very left out.

Mitzi couldn't go to the Wurstelprater. She and Fredl were going to look at an apartment they might rent in a building where a colleague of Fredl lives.

That was fine with me. I wasn't in the mood for the Wurstelprater, anyway. I was even less in the mood to stay home alone. So I put on my "good" brown dress—after all, I had been invited somewhere. And now I had no reason not to go there.

Later

Father L. is just the same, except his hair is partly gray now. I loved seeing him! And Lieselotte's Mutterl was really glad to see me, and of course being together with Lieselotte was fine. But I couldn't enjoy myself so very much, because I kept thinking about O.O. And I wondered what he would think if he knew what sort of reception I was at. I'd rather not write or even think about it now.

When I got back from there, my parents were back from the station and asked where I'd been. "At Anni Hopf's, she invited me over," I said. They believed me.

Monday, March 21

In just one week they have changed the best, or maybe only second-best, girls' *Gymnasium* in Vienna into a place that might as well have Frau Scholz-Klink's motto about the soup ladle carved into the wall above the entrance.

Frau Doktor Waldemar, the founder of this school, to whom it was the most important thing in her whole life, is not director of it anymore. And nobody knows where she is. I heard one rumor that they put her in jail; another, that she died; and still another, that she is safe in Sweden.

A Herr von Hammels, a Berliner, is the director now.

Nazi flags and Hitler portraits hang in all the classrooms. The corridor walls are covered with posters about Strength Through Joy, the B.D.M., the Labor Service, and the new plebiscite. It will be held on April 10. The voting booths won't even have curtains. The Gestapo men or SD men or both will look over people's shoulders, and woe to whoever doesn't vote Yes, in favor of the Anschluss (a little belatedly since it will have been in effect almost a whole month by then!).

English, Latin, and Home Lore have all been eliminated. Instead we have Lore of the Reich. And later in the week we will have National Socialist Ideology, just like in Scholz-Klink, to be taught by Herr Direktor von Hammels himself. I wouldn't be surprised if pretty soon they set up a room with stoves and sinks and we had Housewifely Arts as well.

Physical Education periods have been doubled, with "To the right, march, to the rear, march," etc., and military stuff like that. Rumors say by the end of the week they may be tripled or quadrupled.

What are we Jewish girls doing going to such a school? (Today we were only seven. Helene Barsch is home with a cold. But Susi König won't be back. The Königs left for Switzerland, suddenly, on Saturday. Anni Hopf told me good-bye from her. Anni is very lost without her.) Thea Seligmann said we are like seven (or eight, when Helene comes back) sheep going to a wolf school. "You're exaggerating," Hilde Auerbach replied. "It isn't that bad. No one's done anything to us yet. And besides, we're not the only anti-Nazis in the class." I agreed with her about that.

"Yes, but still, I'd rather go to a different school," said Beate Winternitz. "Even the Jewish *Gymnasium,* unbeliever though I am."

I'd rather too, if it weren't for Lieselotte. And if it weren't for Fräulein Pappenheim. Strict and formal though she is, very much the lofty teacher separated by a vast gap from her lowly students, still, her feelings do show through, and show how fine and decent she is.

When she saw Lieselotte walk into the classroom this morning, Fräulein Pappenheim's face broke into a rare big, warm smile. She always liked Lieselotte a lot and was really glad to see her back.

At first everyone was glad. Lieselotte used to be quite popular. In November, when she moved away, we didn't think that much about politics, and our class wasn't divided into Nazis and non- and anti-Nazis, the way it is now. Well, now the Brigitte-Herta Nazi faction naturally assumed that since Lieselotte had lived in Germany, she would belong with them. They were in for a big surprise.

After roll call Fräulein Pappenheim said, "Will the following students gather their things and stand: Auerbach, Dornenwald, Goldblum, Kreitzer, Roth, Seligmann, and Winternitz. You seven are to move to the last row."

Our classroom has thirty desks. There are only twenty-two girls in our class. So the last row has always been empty.

Eight girls collected their things and stood up: we seven, and Lieselotte.

"What's she doing, is she crazy?" Herta Kröger whispered loudly.

And Brigitte whispered something back with the words "Jew-befriender" in it.

Fräulein Pappenheim rapped for silence. She pointed her pointer at the two of them and said, "You will kindly remember who is in charge of this classroom and refrain from talking unless you are called upon."

We moved to desks in the last row. Lieselotte picked the desk next to mine. Her choosing to sit in that row made it into a place of honor. Not only I, we all thought so.

But then something occurred to me: What if the same thing happens that happened in Scholz-Klink, namely, that she gets into trouble and her father hears about it? I picked up her schoolbag, which she had put down, and handed it to her. I said, "Lieselotte, the gesture's enough. You shouldn't sit here. Think what would hap—"

Fräulein Pappenheim rapped for silence again. "Inge and Lieselotte, I don't recall giving you permission to hold a private conference," she said, not very harshly. And as if she'd overheard what I was thinking, she told Lieselotte, "Now you had better move back to where you were."

Lieselotte moved, and not too soon. The next moment the new Herr Direktor came in on an inspection tour and satisfied himself that everything was proceeding according to the New Order.

During Literature, though we hadn't finished *Nathan the Wise,* Fräulein Pappenheim collected our copies and without a word, with a blank look on her face, dumped them into two big wastepaper baskets. It was quite a change from the usual procedure, whereby she inspects books we return very carefully and charges us fines: ten groschen each for marked-up or dog-eared pages; a schilling for torn pages if they can be pasted; if not, we have to pay the price of a new copy.

Then she passed out copies of *Minna von Barnhelm,* also by Lessing, longer, boring, and with no Jewish characters in it.

Lieselotte and I both had to go home after school. But at least we could walk together part of the way by the route we had worked out this morning, through little courtyards and side streets in which there was no chance or maybe one in a thousand of running into Herr Vessely if he came home at an unexpected hour. We didn't need to worry about Heinz, his school lets out later.

To our surprise, even in the small side streets we took, very narrow, unofficial-looking ones, there were a lot of huge Hitler faces up on posters telling people to vote Yes on the plebiscite. We talked about that on our way home and made up the following astounding news developments for when April 10 draws near: Mussolini decides he'll honor his treaty promises after all, better late than never, and guarantees Austria's borders—retroactively. So then England and France guarantee them also. So do Switzerland, Yugoslavia, Hungary, Czechoslovakia—all the European countries—whether they had treaties with Austria about it or not. And on April 8, or maybe 9, they all send troops, tanks, cannons, whatever they've got. Then they issue a joint ultimatum to Hitler: "Hold the plebiscite! Just make sure it's free and secret, with curtains around the voting booths and nobody snooping around." Then still more astonishing things happen: Certain Nazis, for instance, Herr Vessely, have sudden changes of heart. The others banish themselves back to Germany. And the outcome of the plebiscite is a world-shaking, epoch-making NO, WE DON'T WANT THE ANSCHLUSS! Well, then Hitler has to withdraw with his tail between his legs, the "Ostmark" is Austria again, and everything is fine, Jews and other anti-Nazis come out of jails and places like that, and back from emigrating, and a festival is declared that will go on for a week with free schnitzel and salad and wine and beer and dancing in all the streets.

When I got home, the door to the living room was shut. Mitzi rushed out of the kitchen and greeted me with, "The Devil's grandmother's in there telling your mother bad things about me."

I didn't know whom she meant. Then I saw Usch's muskrat hanging on the coatrack. "Why do you think she's telling things about you?"

"Well, when she handed me her animal to hang up, she said, 'I'd watch my step if I were you, my girl.' Hurry up, go in your room and listen."

"What makes you think I do that?"

"I don't think, I know!"

So I got into my listening position on my bed, and I heard Usch saying the same things she had said to Vati Saturday: She misses Oma Sofie. She has nobody now. Well, maybe just a friend or two. And one of those friends advised her that after all her years of service she ought to be allowed to stay on in the apartment.

"But you can, Usch, till June," my mother said.

"Time passes quickly for people my age, Frau D. In June what will I do?"

"Well, you have your pension, plus some savings, don't you?"

"It's hard to live on that."

Mutti asked her what she wanted.

"The rent money for Frau Dornenwald's apartment for five years."

I heard Mutti draw a whistling breath in through her teeth. "Ten thousand five hundred schillings! Usch, you can't be serious! Even under normal circumstances we couldn't raise so much money! The way things are, we'll be lucky if we can pay all the different taxes and fees the Nazis are imposing on Jews."

"*Gnädige Frau,* I don't understand such complicated things. I'm just a simple woman, a servant, that's all. And speaking of servants, I feel I must warn you, that Mitzi of yours—"

"What about her?"

"On my last visit to this apartment I had the misfortune of seeing with my own two eyes your husband behaving—how shall I put it?—indecorously with her."

My knuckles were white, I gripped my pen so hard. Just write it all down, I told myself, worry about what to believe later!

Mutti laughed. "Usch, that's too ridiculous! What do you mean?"

"I saw the two of them, arm in arm, drinking together—"

"A toast to Mitzi's wedding! Proposed by my father, with all of us present in the room! You can't seriously believe there was anything wrong with that!"

"Frau D., a Jewish man of certain years and a young Aryan girl—"

"*Pfui,* Usch. I'd like to forget you ever said that."

"Frau D., you are forgetting, we Aryans are duty-bound to report any instances of such behavior to our block wardens."

"Oh, for God's sake! Franzi has never done anything dishonorable in his entire life. And you, of all people, know it. You nursed him at your own breast, like a mother."

"A wet nurse, Frau D. That was the custom in those times. Just as now it is the custom to protect the morals of innocent Aryan girls."

"That's enough," my mother said. "Get out of here."

I got it down, as nearly word for word as possible.

Mitzi was wrong: Compared to Usch, the Devil's grandmother is a nice old lady. Usch is more like the person in the story out of whose mouth, when she spoke, jumped toads, wriggled snakes. No, that isn't fair to toads and snakes.

Naturally, I couldn't tell Mitzi. I just said, "Oh, Usch just talked about missing Oma Sofie. You know, how alone she is, etcetera. Nothing about you."

Now I know whom Usch is like: the Basilisk, part rooster, part monstrous giant toad, who is supposed to have lived in the well in front of the Basilisk House in the Schönlaterngasse. Its breath was poisonous fumes, the mere sight of it could kill. The way they got rid of it was somebody brave held a mirror to its face, and it was so shocked by its own appearance, it burst into bits with a loud explosion. I know it doesn't help to wish the same on her. . . .

Vati came home at ten at night for supper. He'd gone to three consulates during the day—I don't know which ones—to ask about temporary visas, without success. So then he'd had to work late at the office.

I was already in bed. I tried not to listen to Mutti telling him about Usch. Hearing it once was enough. But the wall is so thin, I heard it all again.

When he came into my room to say good night, I asked if Usch really meant those things or was only threatening.

He pretended to be more upset about my listening through the wall. He said I misheard everything, and that I should forget it.

Then, though it was so late, he went out again, to see Usch, I heard him tell Mutti, to try and straighten things out, and I got out of bed to write this.

Tuesday, March 22

Today, for a change, some good things happened:

The whole lower school had a volleyball game. One of the captains was a big Nazi from the second-year class. The other captain was Lieselotte, so it was Nazis against non-Nazis, and we won! Thirty-seven to twenty-nine! I got in one really hard serve, I still feel it in my knuckles. It only got us one point. But it hit Herta Kröger in the side, such a wham, she had to sit down and be out of the game for ten minutes.

When I got home from school, Mutti said, "Surprise, look!" The living room was back to normal. The hospital bed was gone. Some men from the rental place came for it this morning. She doesn't need it anymore.

And: I got mail today—from Tommi! A picture postcard of Zagreb with an X showing where they live. He writes that Zagreb is beautiful and he's learning Croatian, which is a tongue-twister language. And he says, "We wish you were here." He wants me to write him back. And he signs it, "Cordially, Tommi."

Cordially—that doesn't just mean "best greetings." That means "from the heart"!

I started to write him back. But strange to say, I, who have filled up almost this whole book, could not think of a single word after "Dear Tommi," and even if I could have, my fingers trembled too much.

Wednesday, March 23

The auditorium of our school is sometimes used for chamber-music concerts or recitals in the evenings. It has pictures on the walls of famous composers.

Well, today we had our first school assembly under the New Order, and there was a big blank space between Schubert and Chopin. They took away Mendelssohn. Of course—he was Jewish! And Gustav Mahler too, for the same reason. A big fancy metal laurel wreath with a metal swastika inside covered the space after Richard Strauss, where I used to gaze at Gustav Mahler's dark wavy hair and intense, stern eyes and noble nose with flaring nostrils.

Whoever picked the honor guard must have had two requirements: big bosoms and B.D.M. uniforms. Six girls from the top class who had those brought in the flag. And all the Aryans said out loud, solemnly, in rhythm, "We are sworn to the flag/For always and ever./Forever accursed be he/Who besmirches the flag."

One lucky thing about being Jewish and excluded is that you get to keep your mouth shut. If I had to say those things,

I'd feel as though toads and snakes were coming out of *my* mouth.

That's how Lieselotte used to feel too, she told me. But then she just invented a kind of switch in her mind. She can flip it on whenever she wants, and it turns stuff like that into rigmarole as meaningless as *rum bum bidi bau wau.*

Speaking of *bau wau,* tomorrow it will be exactly three months since she got Schnackerl. And her father is going to Atzgersdorf on "repatriation" business for the whole day and letting Heinz skip school so he can go with him. So the coast will be clear, and I'm invited to see their apartment and to Schnackerl's celebration. I can hardly wait!

I found a marrow bone, perfectly shaped for gnawing on, in our icebox.

"*Heh,* what are you doing with that? I need it to make soup with," Mitzi said.

But I talked her into donating it for the occasion. I wrapped it in tissue paper and tied it with a red ribbon.

Now, to serious matters:

Some people Mutti has written to abroad have written back already. None are sure they can help us get visas.

Vati has been to more consulates, I forget which all. No luck so far.

As for Usch, my parents don't mention her—like people used to not mention the plague. I don't think Vati got things straightened out with her.

———

Late in the evening

Frau Plattau is here. It's her first visit since Herr Plattau died. She got very thin. She is younger than Mutti, but now she looks about fifty years old.

Vati's right, I shouldn't listen through the wall. Only bad news seems to come through. Vati is talking about the business. It's still called Dornenwald and Plattau. It has a new "manager." The Aryanization Bureau sent him, as boss over Vati. His job is to "smooth the transition." The transition is between now and when the Aryanization Bureau takes the businesses of Jewish owners away from them. The manager is only twenty-three years old. "He's a louse-boy. He knows as much about import-export as I do about training fleas for the flea circus," says Vati to make Frau Plattau smile.

Later

Frau Plattau left. Vati put her in a taxi. Now he's telling Mutti things he couldn't say in front of her: He has to pay the "louse-boy," whose name is Herr Säuberlich, three times the salary he draws himself, and three times the salary Max Plattau drew.

Mutti says, "But that way you'll go bankrupt!"

"Yes, and guess whom the Aryanization Bureau will hold responsible: Me!" Vati also tells her that Herr Säuberlich thinks Max Plattau embezzled money from the business, that that's the reason he killed himself.

Mutti calls Herr Säuberlich a name I've never heard her use, even through the wall. She says, "If the rest of the world were half as honorable as poor old Max was, there wouldn't be any people in it like that —— Herr Säuberlich."

Thursday, March 24

I never got to Schnackerl's celebration. I got into awful trouble instead. I may have gotten us all into awful trouble. . . .

This morning, when I still thought I was going to her house, I showed Lieselotte the marrow bone all wrapped up. She said that was Schnackerl's favorite kind of bone. She told me she had three presents for him: a rubber bone, a ball with a bell inside, and a soft brush to brush him with after baths.

When finally the last bell rang, we were the first ones out the school door.

Out there, waiting, stood my father. "Ingelein, surprise!" He came toward us, smiling. He extended his hand and asked, "Aren't you going to introduce me to your friend?"

"Vati"—it was hard to get the words out— "don't you remember?"

Yes, oh, yes, now he did. His face went furious. The vein in his forehead stood out. He let his hand fall to his side.

"Herr Dornenwald, *Grüss Gott*," said Lieselotte in a small voice.

My father, that polite man, turned his back on her. He grabbed me by the wrist and pulled. "No, wait!" I pulled in the other direction. "I have to give her something."

He pulled harder, of course. I had to follow. I couldn't give her the marrow bone.

Vati, I hate you. The words beat inside me, as loud as my heart beat, as loud as my shoe soles on the sidewalk pavement.

After a while he let go of my wrist. I trudged behind him, I don't know how long, across the Kohlmarkt, past St. Peter's, in silence.

We came to the Tuchlauben, the street his office is on. We came to the building. He stopped and pointed at the door. There was always a brass sign there: DORNENWALD AND PLATTAU, IMPORT-EXPORT. It was gone. Now there was a new sign: IMPORT-EXPORT, FRIEDRICH SÄUBERLICH, MANAGER.

"I didn't intend to show you that," said Vati. "I meant to give myself a treat, surprise you, take you out for midday meal. . . ." He kept his eyes on the sign. His shoulders slumped now that he was standing still. The rest of him slumped too, even his voice.

I took it back about hating him. I didn't anymore. I just felt awful—for him, for me, for Lieselotte, and because of everything.

He put his finger on my chin and raised my face up. We stood like that a moment: he looking at the misery on my face; I, at the misery on his.

"You must be hungry," he said.

I wasn't. But I didn't want to say no to him just then. So I nodded. We went into a small restaurant down the street.

I don't remember what we ordered. Whatever it was, we hardly touched it. Instead we talked.

I started. I told him how wrong he is, how wrong he has

always been, about Lieselotte. I told him that she is not a Nazi; and about her father beating her; and about her moving to the last row with us; and what a wonderful, loyal, brave friend she is, has always been, to me.

He listened to it all. He only interrupted me once, by putting his finger over his lips, meaning I should talk more softly so no one would overhear. When I was done, I felt sure I had convinced him.

He granted me that Lieselotte is a fine, good person. He even said he doesn't blame me anymore for having stayed her friend. "But, Inge, you must realize what you are doing." He paused. His blue, blue eyes looked into mine. I looked for the start of a smile in his. There was no hint of one.

"What am I doing, Vati?"

"You are endangering our lives."

My breath caught in my throat.

"Don't you see, Inge? Must I spell it out for you? A man like Herr Vessely, an officer in the SA—who, as you say, beat his own daughter with his belt across her back! If he found out she still 'befriends' Jews, he'd stop at nothing to 'unbefriend' them, believe me!"

"But, Vati, that's exactly why we're so careful." I told him about our telephone system and about the secret route we take through back streets and courtyards.

"That's all childishness, Inge. Just think, what if Herr Vessely had decided to pick up his daughter from school by surprise? What if *he'd* seen the two of you? That could have happened just as easily. That could happen tomorrow! I'll tell you what he'd do. He'd save Usch the trouble of slandering me to the block warden. He'd save Herr Säuberlich the trouble of reporting me to the Aryanization Bureau for not being an alchemist, which would be the only way I could produce enough money to save the business from his idiocy and greed. Herr Vessely could give a very simple order and rid himself once and for all of the embarrassment of his daughter's befriending a Jewess. Our doorbell would ring at five or six the next morning. And this time the SA would not be so kind as to escort me—all of us—back home again. I'm not making this up to frighten you. And you don't have to say anything. Just think about it. That's all I ask."

I thought about it harder than anything in my whole life before. I'm still thinking about it, very hard. And I'm coming up with nothing but no's: No, I cannot go on "endangering our lives." No, I cannot talk about this with Lieselotte. Well then, no, I can't face her either. I don't see how I can face going to school tomorrow.

Friday, March 25

My parents let me stay home.

I did useful things:

I helped Mutti with the lists she has been making of everything we own. I listed how many different-sized lace and plain tablecloths and napkins we have. I separated out half a dozen not too big or fancy ones and matching napkins. We'll pack those and take those with us if we can bring enough suitcases. That will depend on what country we get visas for.

Then Mitzi sent me down for onions, dill, and parsley.

The greengrocer is on the Löwengasse, across from my old school.

When I'd bought the vegetables, I crossed the street and stood outside the iron fence, gazing through the bars into the school yard. I saw chalk marks on the ground. Some little girl had disobeyed and had probably gotten scolded. I started reminiscing about Lieselotte and me in there when we were little. . . .

While I stood there Herr Mühlenbach, the white-haired old hunched-over school janitor, opened the doors. Why? I wondered. It was only a quarter to eleven! School couldn't be letting out yet. Then why did little girls come out, single file, schoolbags on their backs?

First came four really small ones. I'd forgotten how like babies girls in the first class look. One was quiet. One was crying noisily, and two, medium loud.

Then came five from the second class, two crying, three looking about to.

Another thing I wondered was, Why did Herr Mühlenbach, who always used to pat our heads when he saw us cry, look so stony-faced?

Then came the third- and fourth-class girls. Next to last came Evi. She was almost as bent-over as Herr Mühlenbach, as though her schoolbag weighed a thousand kilos, and she stared down at the stone steps.

"Psst, Evi!"

"Inge! How come you're here? Did you know?"

"I was just at the greengrocer's. Did I know what?" But by then I was starting to guess.

"From now on this school is just for Aryans," said Evi. "We have to go to a Jew school. In the Second District, on the Erdberggasse. And you know what else? Frau Willauer" (her teacher, whom she adores) "didn't even say good-bye to us!"

"Evi, don't feel bad. Maybe you'll like the new school. In any case, just think, you won't have to sit in the last row."

"Every row will be the last row there," said Evi.

I said, "That's silly." But I knew what she meant.

Her mother wasn't home, she didn't have the key to their apartment, and for once she didn't want to play Heaven and Hell in the courtyard. So she came to our apartment, and we played War, a boring card game, till she could go home.

Sunday night, March 27

For the first time since I started writing in here again, the day I went to temple with O.O., I've let two whole days go by without opening this book. A lot has happened. But I haven't had the heart to write about it.

I didn't go to school yesterday either. How could I have looked Lieselotte in the eye, how will I ever be able to, and say, Listen, I convinced my father that you are the best, the truest friend, and he convinced me that by spending time with you I'm endangering my parents' lives, and mine, so let's pretend we don't know each other, all right?

Instead of school, I thought I'd go to temple. Oh, not because

I've suddenly become religious. It's just that along with everything else, I've been thinking about O.O. a lot, missing him, that's all.

When I got to the Seitenstette, the temple was barred shut and a sign on the door said CLOSED UNTIL FURTHER NOTICE. Two SS men in black uniforms with black boots on strutted back and forth in front of it. So I went home again.

On our street I met Herr and Frau Fried. I said *"Grüss Gott"* to them and I asked, "Did Evi go to the new school today, or is it closed on account of Sabbath?"

Frau Fried made a strange noise in her throat. Herr Fried took her arm. She covered her face with her other arm. "We just put Evi on the train," said Herr Fried. "She's going to France, from there to England—"

"By herself?" I asked.

"The conductor is keeping an eye on her. In England we have third cousins. She will stay with them a short while. Then she will go to Manchuria. We have close relatives there. They can take Evi in, but not all three of us."

Close! How can they be close, in Manchuria? That's the farthest-away place in the world!

"We hope we can arrange to go there ourselves, eventually." The way he said *eventually,* it sounded like "next to never."

"How come she didn't tell me? I saw her yesterday, and she didn't say a word!"

"She didn't know," said Herr Fried. "We didn't want to worry her ahead of time. We only told her this morning."

Just like when she had her tonsils out, only then, she woke up and it was over. And now, soon, she'll be at the other end of the world, but her parents will still be here!

"At least we know she's safe," Frau Fried said.

Safe! Safe is when you are with your parents. A picture came into my mind of Evi, all alone, looking over the railing of a ship in the middle of the China Sea, or the Sea of Japan, or some other ocean so far away, I don't even know its name.

"Excuse me"—a sick feeling came into my throat—"I have to hurry, my mother's waiting for me." I broke into a run, I ran from them, from what they'd done and from their miserable faces.

"Mutti! Mutti!" I shouted when I got in the door. But she was not waiting for me. I looked in the living room, the bedroom, the study, all over.

"Why are you tearing around like that, yelling for your mother like a baby? She's out," said Mitzi. "Be glad she can go out again."

"Where did she go?"

"To your father's office. The bookkeeper quit. Or the secretary. I don't know which. In any case, your mother's helping out there."

I hung around Mitzi all day the way I used to when I was little.

Finally my parents came home, both really tired. Mutti went to their bedroom to lie down.

Vati collapsed on the living-room couch with the newspaper.

"Listen, Vati, I have to tell you something."

He put the paper aside. I started to tell him about Evi. I was sitting on the edge of the couch. In the middle of a sentence I suddenly thought of an old game we used to play. It was called Hop and Bop. Vati would lie with his knees up and say, "Inge, hop!" I'd hop onto his knees. He'd let me sit there. We'd smile at each other as though nothing were going to happen. Then suddenly he'd yell, "Bop!" Down would go his knees, and I'd drop to the couch and bounce there, laughing wildly.

I finished telling about Evi.

"Poor little girl," my father said. "May she get there safely."

"Vati, can you imagine her parents doing such a terrible thing, sending her that far away, on her own?"

"Inge, think how hard it must be on them too. They must have decided to do that because they have no other choice, no chance of escaping anywhere all together."

"Vati, listen, will we—"

I didn't have to finish the question. He said, "Inge, I promise you I'll do everything in my power to make sure that when we leave, we leave as a family."

His saying that made me feel even sorrier for Evi. But it made me feel better about him and me. Or I couldn't have written all this.

Today was the last Sunday morning before the wedding. Fredl came over to pick Mitzi up. They wanted me to go to church with them, because after the service they were going to rehearse walking down the aisle.

I wanted to go. But I thought, What if Lieselotte is there? Facing her, there, in the church without a swastika, which we never would have known about if not for her, would be even more impossible! So I said, "No, I can't."

Fredl winked at me. "I know the feeling." He thought I just didn't want to.

"How will she know what to do, then, Friday?" said Mitzi.

"Well now, let's see." Fredl touched his finger to his forehead to show that he was thinking deeply. "I have it! We'll show her where the aisle is, in case she can't find it for herself. Then she'll put her right foot in front of her left, and her left in front of her right, and so forth, and so forth, and—miracle!—she'll end up in front of the altar, right behind you. How about that?"

"Oh, you," said Mitzi, and they went.

During breakfast, using Oma Sofie's key again, Usch walked in on us. She really doesn't look like the monster Basilisk. She's really just an average, not bad-looking, not even especially mean-looking, tallish, broadly built elderly woman. She said, "I didn't want to disturb." Well, she disturbed, and how!

She sat down but wouldn't take her "animal" off. She said, "I came here straight from church. The sermon made me realize it's my duty as a Christian and as a Reich citizen to settle, er, you-know-what quickly. But perhaps you would rather not discuss this in front of the child."

Vati said—it made me realize how much things have changed between us—"Don't you worry about Inge. Inge can stay."

Usch wants nine thousand, five hundred schillings. She has come down a thousand schillings since she talked to Mutti. For nine thousand, five hundred, she would be willing to shut her eyes, retroactively, to what took place between Vati and Mitzi.

"Why not a million?" Mutti said.

"If that is how you feel, Frau D., I had better go." Usch stood up.

"Wait," said Vati. "Be realistic. I could perhaps raise—let, me see—two thousand schillings, at the very most. But with all the forms that must be filled out before one can withdraw money from banks nowadays, it would take at least a week."

Usch said no. That would be too late and far too little. She already has an appointment with the block warden. She told us his name: Herr Dieter Knorr. "Oh, by the way," she added, "he is a *Hauptsturmführer* in the SS." She made the appointment for next Friday. "I'm giving you five days."

"Thank you very much," said Mutti. "There is something else I would like you to 'give' us." She held out her hand. "The key to this apartment, please."

Usch gave it to her and left. This time Vati did not see her out.

"Well, now at least she can't drop in on us again," I said.

"We can't count on that," said Mutti. "She could have had another key made."

"Why can't Mitzi go to that block warden too?" I asked. "Why can't she just tell him it's all not true?"

"Because under the New Order, 'justice' doesn't work that way. She'd just be labeled 'Jew-befriender' and bring trouble on herself," said my father.

"What are we going to do?"

"Get out, and fast," said Mutti.

"How? Where will we go?"

Vati ran his hand through his hair. "God knows."

Mutti said, "Franzl, don't sound like that! We have to, and we will, by hook or by crook." She'd gotten up from the table and pulled him up too. "Let's start by making some telephone calls, long distance. Entrance regulations change every day. Who knows, if your sister knew how urgent it was, she might be able to do something. Or maybe that Herr What's-his-name from Prague, with whom you did business. Let's try, come on."

They went to the study. "Inge, you stay out, please," said my mother. "It's hard enough to make such calls. We need privacy."

Yes, I could understand that. I cleared and washed the break-fast dishes. But after that I thought, I need to know what's going on even more than they need privacy.

So I went in there too.

I could tell just by the look on Mutti's face she was waiting to be connected with the Löwbergs in Zagreb.

"Hannerl, be careful," my father said. "I heard clicks before. I'm sure the long-distance lines are tapped."

Mutti described our situation, in a roundabout way, to Uncle Herbert. Then she waited. Aunt Marianne came on. Mutti said, "Hello, Mariandl, how are you—what?" and she looked very surprised. Then I think Uncle Herbert came back on. Mutti lis-tened, smiling, looking happier and happier. "Thank you, thank you, dear good friend, yes, oh, I hope so!" She hung up.

"Well?" Vati asked excitedly.

Uncle Herbert knows a man in Zagreb who owns a textile fac-tory like the one Vati's father, Opa Moritz, had, at which my father worked before he went into the import-export business with Max Plattau. Uncle Herbert thinks he might be able to get this man to give Vati a job. On the strength of that we might be able to get visas. Uncle Herbert is going to visit the man right now and ask. He will let us know what develops.

"Wonderful!" said Vati. "What did Marianne say?"

Mutti frowned. "She told me—twice!—how 'comforting' it is to be a Christian, how safe it makes one feel in these times."

Vati laughed. "Our Marianne said that? The most outspoken atheist in our circle?"

"She's trying to tell us something," Mutti said.

"What? That we should be baptized? I doubt it. She knows our feelings too well. Besides, if that could solve anything, people would be trying it by the thousands. I haven't heard of anybody doing it. Have you?"

"No," said Mutti.

"I have. Listen, Mutti, Vati, I have to tell you something. Last week, the day O.O. left, I went to—"

"Inge, please, not now! Can't you see we're busy? Where's the telephone book? We have important things to do!" She looked up a number. She told it to Vati. He dialed and spoke to a lawyer. He asked whether people whom someone denounces to a block warden are entitled to any sort of defense. The answer was clearly no.

"Now leave us alone," said Mutti, and I went out of the room.

In less than an hour Uncle Herbert called back. The factory owner said yes! Uncle Herbert is sending a telegram that Vati can show at the consulate.

My parents feel very optimistic that it's going to work out.

———

Monday, March 28

I wrote all that last might, waiting for Mitzi to get back from her day off. She finally did, at a quarter past one.

I called her into my room.

"Still up, night owl?"

"Mitzi, do me a favor!"

"What?

"Show me your wedding gown."

"No! I already told you, that brings bad luck."

"The bad luck already came. If you don't show it to me, I won't see it."

"Baloney. You'll see it Friday."

"No, Mitzi. Sit here." She sat down on my bed. "We'll be gone by then. If not—"

"If not, what?"

"Something awful, I can't tell you. You just have to believe me. Cross your fingers we'll get out! We have to!"

She crossed, not her fingers, her whole self, like in church. "All right. I'll be back."

My small bed lamp was the only light on. So when she came back, standing in the door in the half dark, she looked shimmery, the way I used to imagine my guardian angel when I still believed I had one. And when she came nearer, taking dignified, slow steps, moving more gracefully than I've ever seen her do, she looked like a dancer in a ballet. When she stood by my bed, I saw the different materials of the dress: Only the skirt of it shimmers. That's made of satin and has tiny seed pearls sewn on. The bodice is of handmade lace. And the veil is as fine as the threads in a spider web. And the train is so long, she had to drape it over her arm.

I filled my eyes with it, I looked and looked.

"Well? Aren't you going to say anything?"

"Oh, Mitzi, it's a dream!"

"No, it's not. Get up, sloth. If you can't do it on Friday like you're supposed to, you can carry my train right now!"

It swished as she arranged it in my hands. "There. Now, sing that march, you know the one."

"From *Lohengrin*?"

"Yes, that one."

I did. And we walked, she in front, I holding up the train, carefully, carefully, for not one speck from the floor must get on it, around the room three times in all solemnity and festive-ness.

"There. Now get back into bed. That's just how it will be. So when it's happening, you'll know, wherever you are," Mitzi said gruffly. Then she sobbed out, "Safe from harm, please God!" And she threw herself across my bed and cried her eyes out.

"Mitzi, stop! You're rumpling the dress. You're getting it wet."

"You're right." She sat up. She wiped her face on my eider-down. Then she kissed me. Then, in her gruff voice again, she asked, "Who's going to be my bridesmaid?"

And I said, "Don't worry. I'll get one for you."

Around dawn I heard the doorbell. First I thought it was part of a nightmare I was having. But no, it really rang. So then I thought, Oh, God, the SA.

Vati went to the door. He was white in the face, he was scared too.

But it was the telegram!

TEXTILE FACTORY POSITION, GUARANTEED TO GOSPODIN FRANZ DORNENWALD STOP CONSUL INVITED TO CONFIRM WITH GOSPODIN LAVRIC COMMA OWNER COMMA LAVRIC TEXTILES AT PODSUSED COMMA ZAGREB OUTSKIRTS STOP HEARTY GREETINGS STOP

CHRISTIAN LÖWBERG

"*Christian* Löwberg?" I asked.

"Telegraph operators can make mistakes," Vati said.

But *Herbert* and *Christian* don't sound a bit alike. I didn't think that could be a mistake. Later I found out Mutti didn't think so either. . . .

"I can't bear to go to school, I have to know what will happen," I begged my parents. They let me go with them to the consulate.

On the way Mutti needed cigarettes. She and Vati went into a tobacconist's.

Outside the shop was a *Stürmer* display case with this week's edition of the *Stürmer*. On the front page was the usual ugly pot-bellied Jew with snot dripping out of his huge hooked nose. The headlines were: A HUNDRED JEWISH SUICIDES DAILY NOT ENOUGH. THOUSANDS NEEDED. GOERING CALLS FOR JEW-CLEANSED VIENNA.

"*Pfui*, Inge, don't look at that filth," Mutti said, coming out of the store, and they pulled me away.

When it was our turn, Vati went in to see the consul. Mutti and I waited in the waiting room.

He came quickly out again. There is a lot of unemployment in Yugoslavia, the consul had told him. Why should a foreigner be let in who'd take a job away from a Yugoslav citizen?

Vati shrugged and looked grim. "Now I'd better hurry to my office, I mean, Herr Säuberlich's office, or he will report me for business neglect, and then the Ayranization Bureau can race Usch's block warden for who ruins us first. Hannerl, you're worn out. Inge, take her home. In a taxi, so she won't have to walk any extra steps." And he left.

But Mutti wasn't ready. She looked at her face in her pocket mirror. She moved her hat to a more becoming angle, put powder on her nose, dabbed a little rouge on her cheeks. "Now *I'm* going to see the consul. You come too."

The consul greeted us politely and helped her into a chair.

"Forgive us for taking still more of your time, Gospodin Consul. I just wanted to inquire about visiting your lovely country for a short vacation. You see, I have this annoying condition"—she pointed to her hip and cane— "and my doctor thinks the best cure would be a week or so by the balmy Adriatic."

"But, *Gnädige Frau,* your husband spoke about moving there permanently."

My mother gave a rippling, forced laugh. "Oh, that's a foolish whim of his. He knows perfectly well I won't consider moving away. Why, Vienna is my home, and always will be." She took out a Memphis.

The consul came out from behind his desk and lit it for her. "Thank you so much."

"But, er, if you don't mind my asking, aren't you and your husband Jew—er, well, perhaps I misunderstood."

"Jewish?" She sounded surprised. Then, "Oh, I understand, you saw our passports, and of course they are stamped 'Jewish.' No, no"—she gave the ripply laugh again, and this time it made me shiver— "we are Catholic. We just didn't think to bring along our baptismal certificates. After all, one is not in the habit of carrying around all one's documents." She smiled at him.

He smiled back and made an inviting gesture with his hands. "*Gnädige Frau,* my country welcomes you. By all means, go and travel there. Provided, er—"

"Provided what?"

"Provided your baptismal certificates are dated 1936 or earlier."

Mutti's smile froze. "Thank you." And we left.

"You should have been an actress," I said when we were out of there. "That was a good performance."

"Well, I had to find out. And now I know." She leaned hard on her cane, as if she couldn't hold herself up any longer. "It's hopeless."

"No, it's not. Taxi!"

One came. We got in. Mutti gave the driver our address. Then she took her hat off and put her head back against the seat. Her face was crumpled up from all the smiles she had put on.

"Mutti, please, don't look so hopeless!" I moved close to her and whispered into her ear, "Remember when you took O.O. to the train? That day I went to a reception for some people who'd just been baptized."

"Oh? You don't say? Why?"

"Because Lieselotte—"

"Stop! I don't want to hear about her. I thought your father made you realize, finally, that with that friendship of yours you're risking—"

"That was before! Mutti, you have to listen! She invited me to her uncle's rectory. He's a priest. He was the religion teacher in my old school who was so nice to me, remember?" I whispered his name into her ear. (I'm not writing it in here anymore, secret though I keep this book.) "His church is the one that didn't fly the swastika when Hitler came. And, you see, his housekeeper has lumbago, so Lieselotte's mother—she's his sister—and Lieselotte were helping serve coffee and cake and things. And the reason Lieselotte invited me is, it was a chance to see each other—"

"You didn't feel the need to tell me all this then. Why now?"

"Because, listen: One of the people, a lady about your age, said something to him, and I just thought . . . Well, anyway, she said, 'Father L., you are a saint.' That embarrassed him. So she said, 'All right, if not a saint, then a dear, good sorcerer. For who else could make the time turn back?'"

Mutti sat up. "And you thought—"

"I didn't think anything, then. But you see, the people who'd been baptized went into his study one by one and were alone in there and came out with their certificates. So when the consul said that about 1936 or before, it made me think maybe Father L. let them fill in the dates themselves."

Mutti drew her breath in through her teeth and whispered, "Your word in God's ear!" Then she leaned forward and said, "Driver, we've changed our minds, we want to go somewhere else. Inge, tell him where."

Father L. came to the door. He didn't act surprised, didn't ask why I wasn't in school.

"Father L., this is my mother."

"Frau Dornenwald, it's a pleasure." He shook hands and invited us in.

He took our coats. We went into his study. We sat down. Mutti's hands shook. I handed her her pocketbook. "It's all right to smoke," I said.

Father L. brought her an ashtray. He took his pipe out of a table drawer and started filling it in a leisurely way.

The oddest feeling came over me. Here we sat, Mutti and I, in, of all places, a rectory, opposite a priest in a black cassock. Yet, instead of feeling out of place, I felt—well, not at home, exactly, but almost. Anyway, comfortable, glad I'd come. I'd felt the same way the Sunday of the reception, even though I'd so clearly not been a part of the occasion. And back in the first class, in Father L.'s classroom by mistake, I'd felt that way too, at least until I tried, and couldn't, call him "Father."

I don't think the feeling has anything to do with his being a Catholic priest. I think he just happens to be the kind of person who can make people feel that way.

Mutti relaxed too. Her hands stopped shaking. I don't know whether she felt the way I did. It may have been just the cigarette steadying her. Anyway, she told him our situation, beginning with Usch (of course not by name) and ending with what the Yugoslav consul had said. And she asked whether he thought he could help us.

He thought so. He gave her two books, one thin, bound in red, and one thicker, in black. The thin one was the catechism; the thicker one, the New Testament. He said usually people take instructions for a few weeks, but since she and my father didn't have that much time, they should read as much as they could. And he would gladly baptize them whenever. "How would tomorrow be?"

"You are wonderfully kind. But Father L."—her voice grew tight and anxious— "I feel I should tell you, by conviction my husband and I are—"

"Please." He made a motion with his hand asking her to hush. He pulled on his pipe. It had gone out, though. "I have my convictions too," he said, relighting it. "For instance, I'm convinced that baptism, along with the other sacraments, is a gift from God, and that it's my job to bestow those gifts, not to withhold them. Besides, Frau Dornenwald"—he puffed, the pipe was drawing well now—"I'll tell you something you may think strange. You may even think it's mumbo jumbo: I think—we think—the sacraments have a power in them. You think so too, though in a different way of course"—he smiled at her, and at me, as though the three of us were sharing a joke— "or else you wouldn't be here."

"True. But—"

"Please, I'm not quite finished. Whatever your convictions are, can you be sure they will never change? Frau Dornenwald, don't misunderstand me. I'm not saying they will change, or even that they should. But if they simply do someday, will you then be quite, quite sure the power I'm talking about had nothing at all to do with bringing the change about?"

Mutti smiled. "I see what you mean."

Her and Vati's appointment is for three o'clock tomorrow. Starting then, I'll be the only person in our immediate family who is officially Jewish. It's funny: When I was little, I wished so hard I could be Catholic like everybody else. And now I'm glad that the law forbids people my age to be baptized. No, it's not that I've turned Jewish-religious. I'm just glad to stay Jewish, that's all.

Later

At first, when Mutti told him, Vati couldn't believe it. Then they started to quarrel.

Vati said, "My father would turn over in his grave if he knew."

"But he won't know," said Mutti. "You think it's easy for me? *My* father will know. Think how he'll feel!"

I knew they would tell me not to mix in. But I'd been thinking about O.O. very hard. I knew how he'd feel. I *had* to tell them. "O.O. would say you did right."

"Don't talk about things you don't understand," Mutti snapped. "Your father and I brought you up without religion. But *my* father was brought up differently. You have no idea what being Jewish means to him."

"Yes, I do. We talked about it. He would tell you what he told me."

"And what was that?" Mutti asked, as though she thought I wouldn't get it right.

Let me not garble this, I hoped so hard, I almost prayed. And I said, "He'd say there are lots of different ways of being Jewish."

"That may be," said Vati, "but getting baptized is hardly one of them."

I forget exactly how I put the next part of what I had to say. Something like, "That depends. If getting baptized saves your lives, and mine too because mine depends on yours, then it is more Jewish."

"That's absurd," said Mutti.

"Yes, but when you're dead, you're nothing. You told me that yourself when Opa Moritz died, don't you remember, Vati? So being something, being anything, being alive, is more Jewish than being nothing, you have to admit!"

I was terribly serious. But something about the way I said all that made them smile.

"You're in philosophical deep waters," said Vati.

"Maybe I am. Or else it's a paradox. Jewish history is full of paradoxes. I'm not just saying that, Rabbi Taglicht said that."

"All right. You can stop arguing now," Vati said.

"You mean you agree?"

They said, "Yes."

Mutti gave a little laugh. "And if—*when* we see O.O. again, you can explain it to him. All right?"

"All right. And he'll understand, you'll see."

Tuesday, March 29

A week ago I couldn't have imagined that I would argue for all I am worth in favor of something that would mean our leaving here before April Fools'. But I did. And I won.

So now, instead of my being Mitzi's bridesmaid on Friday, she and Fredl are my parents' witnesses—or godparents, if grown-ups have those, I don't know.

And here's another paradox: I do feel comfortable around Father L.; and I know my parents are doing the right, the only, thing they can do. Still, I didn't want to be there with them when it happened.

Besides, this is my last private afternoon in my room. Tomorrow we pack. The day after tomorrow we leave, at seven thirty in the morning.

The last thing I will do, when we're already at the Südbahnhof, just before we get on the train, is: I will find a telephone booth, and I will call up Lieselotte. I'll ask her to be Mitzi's bridesmaid. I know she'll say yes. And I'll tell her good-bye. I'm sure she'll still be home. It will be at eight fifteen. She always leaves her house at twenty past.

I can't, I mustn't, talk to her till then. Vati convinced me of that. Because if Herr Vessely found out and got really angry, he could still make everything go wrong for us—and not just for us; for Father L. also, and for the other people he has helped. . . .

———

Later

I don't know what I expected—certainly not shimmering haloes over my parents' heads! They look exactly the same as before.

Everything went fine. The baptismal certificates are in order—or rather, not in order, depending on how you look at it. Oh, well, *I* know what I mean.

Vati has just gone to ask Herr Listopat for the key to the storage attic, where tenants' trunks and suitcases are kept.

Still later

We were in the study. My parents were clearing out papers. I was looking through our two-dozen photograph albums—they had given me the job of choosing the three best albums to take along!—when the telephone rang.

Vati was nearest to it and he answered, "Herr Dornenwald," the way he always does. Then his voice rose: "Anni Hopf?"

"Give it to me!" I reached for the receiver.

He held on to the receiver and said, "No, you're not Anni Hopf, you're Lieselotte Vessely."

"Let *me* talk!" I pulled on his arm.

Mutti pulled me away. "No, let *him*."

"I'm glad you called, Lieselotte," said my father. "I want to apologize for being so rude to you last Thursday. . . . Thank you, that's very gracious of you. Now, here's Inge." He gave me the receiver.

"Hello, Inge, where've you been? I haven't seen you in so

long! Were you sick? Are you all right now? Inge, are you even there?"

I felt as though I had a waterfall inside me, only instead of falling it was pushing up, into my chest, my throat, already it was coming into my eyes. "Lieselotte, is your father home? Is Heinz?" I managed to say.

"No, they went to Graz! They won't be back till Sunday. I can talk now."

"But I can't!" By then I was crying all over the telephone. "I'll call you later." I hung up.

"Why are you crying like that?" Vati asked. He looked hurt. He thought I didn't appreciate that he'd apologized to Lieselotte.

I did, I do! That had touched me very much. In fact, it started me crying. And then, suddenly, when I heard Lieselotte's voice, it hit me that we are leaving forever. It hadn't felt real till that moment.

I tried to explain this to my parents, and they understood.

Then Vati asked, "Now would you like to know what made me talk as I did to Lieselotte?"

"Yes."

"Well, I thought to myself, Inge has behaved politely and respectfully to Usch all these years, and look what Usch is ready to do to us; whereas I've behaved like a lout to Inge's friend—to whom, in a way, we'll owe getting out if all goes well from here on." Now *he* was crying. Not with a gush, like me. His eyes just got a little wet. But that has never happened before, at least not in front of me.

"Vati, listen, her father and her brother are away in Graz! She called to tell me that. And they won't be back till Sunday. We'll be gone by then! So can I call her back now? Can I tell her we're leaving? Can I see her?"

They said "Yes" and went out of the room.

"Hello, Lieselotte? It's me. Listen, can you be Mitzi's bridesmaid on Friday?"

"But I thought you—"

"I can't. We'll be gone by then. Lieselotte, don't ask me anything, let's not talk about it, all right? Just tell me if you can."

"Yes, I think so, yes, I'm sure—"

"Good, that's wonderful."

"But Inge—"

"Listen, we already had one parting last November, and we gave each other presents and cried and so forth. I don't want that again, do you?"

"No—"

"All right. So tomorrow, can you meet me at the Praterstern? At two o'clock?"

Lieselotte said yes, she can!

Wednesday night, March 30

From the Praterstern it's only a short walk to the Wurstelprater. O.O. was right: That's the place to go.

I still had the money he gave me. Lieselotte had money too. We had more than enough for everything. We spent the whole afternoon there.

We gave the *Watschevinann* such smacks, our hands hurt, but who cared? It felt great watching the strength indicator zoom.

We went on almost all the rides. We started with the tame ones, the merry-go-round, the miniature cars and boats. Then we went on the medium-thrilling ones, like the caterpillar and the one with little airplanes; and then on the really wild ones, like the scrambler and the high roller coaster.

While we were on the merry-go-round, bouncing up and down, Lieselotte on a lion, I on a giraffe, the calliope played a lively old tune that stuck in our ears like an earwig. The words to it started like this:

Whom God would favor, those he sends out
To wander in the wide, wide world.

I don't know how the real words continue, I just know—every Viennese knows—the parody:

He lets them bite into a knockwurst
And grants them hearty appetite!

Those words don't make sense, but that's the fun of it, and we sang it and sang it to our hearts' content, so loud, some people smiled and others looked at us and clicked their tongues.

Then we got hungry and had *Würstel* with sauerkraut and mustard and drank *Kracherl,* Lieselotte, a raspberry one, I, grape.

Then we watched the puppet theater. It was just the same as when we were small: Kasperl bopped the policeman over the head, and everybody laughed. Then when the crocodile approached and Kasperl didn't see it, the little children in the audience screamed, "Kasperl, look out!" And when Kasperl escaped, everybody cheered, including us.

Lieselotte said, "Isn't it amazing that with all the real things happening to us, we still care so much what happens to Kasperl?"

I said, "Yes." I knew exactly what she meant.

We saved the Giant Ferris Wheel for last. It's not really part of the Wurstelprater. It's not just a ride, it is also a dignified monument. It was one of the first Ferris wheels ever built, and it's the second most famous landmark of Vienna.

You can see St. Stephen's from it, of course; you can see all the spires and green and gilded domes, and all the rooftops and chimneystacks of the city. You can see the Danube (so greenish gray!) and the Danube bridges; and in the other direction, the Wienerwald and the mountains Kahlenberg and Kobenzl. And if the day is fairly clear, like today was, you can see all the way to the Schneeberg, with eternal snow on its peak.

Earlier we'd bought balloons. Mine was blue, Lieselotte's was green. When we got to the top of the Ferris wheel, I suddenly felt like releasing mine. Not all the compartments have windows that open, but ours did. I put my balloon out the window and let it go. Lieselotte let hers go too. They went sailing out into the sky.

Lieselotte said, "They look like our friendship floating away."

I said, "No, they're just balloons. They just have helium in them, not blood."

"That's true," said Lieselotte.

We linked arms. We watched the balloons float farther and farther away. Then we couldn't see them anymore. But our arms were still linked.

We looked at each other. And we stuck to our agreement, neither of us cried.

"B.S.L. forever," Lieselotte said.

I was thinking the same thing, so I said it too. And we laughed because it sounded so silly, and yet we meant it, we mean it, from the bottoms of both our hearts.

"Besides," I said, "our friendship is in a book now. O.O. gave it to me last Chanukah. All the pages were blank. Now they're almost all filled up. It's about other things too. But mostly it's about how I 'really and truly' feel about you. And about things we've done together. It has your letters in it also."

"I wish I could read it," Lieselotte said.

"I wish you could too. Maybe someday you will."

When I got home, all the packing was done, but in such a way that if someone dropped in on us by surprise—Usch, for instance—she wouldn't notice. Everything we are taking with us is in four suitcases. Three are under my parents' bed. One is under mine. Mitzi will take care of everything that is not packed. She has all the lists Mutti made. So when the man from the storage and shipping place comes, she will tell him what to store and ship to us later. Lots of things, for instance the rug and all the study furniture except the desk, and a spare set of dishes, some pots, pans, glasses, flower vases, and linens Mutti talked her into accepting for her and Fredl's household. The people from the storage place are also movers and will move those things to their new apartment.

After supper I went into Mitzi's room. I'd already told her that Lieselotte will be her bridesmaid. I said, "She'll fill it out better than me on top. I just want to see it one more time."

"What are you jabbering about? And what are you poking around for in my wardrobe?"

"The bridesmaid's dress."

"You think a girl like Lieselotte doesn't have dresses of her own?" Mitzi yelled, really loud. "You think I'd give that dress away to anybody? And who do you think will make you another such dress where you're going? And what do you think you'll wear if that Tommi Löwberg invites you to a dance or someplace fine and fancy? It's in your suitcase. I packed it myself."

That's all I can write tonight. I have to save the last pages for tomorrow.

Thursday, March 31

I stood in the corridor of the train where the view is better and looked out till we came to the suburbs and I couldn't see Vienna anymore. "Vienna, Vienna, you alone/ Shall be the city of my dreams." That old song came into my head, only into my head, not into my feelings. I'm not sad to be leaving Vienna behind. Oh, sure, it's where I was born, and where my parents were born—and if we were not getting out, it's also where we might die. I don't mean when we're old, I mean a lot sooner.

Then I went into our compartment. It's elegant, first class, as if we were still well-off people and only going on vacation. The seats are upholstered in dark-red plush with lace antimacassars to lean one's head against, and there is a table for eating or playing cards on. We have round-trip tickets to a place called Ragusa and back, and reservations for a two-week stay at a beautiful hotel with marble columns and verandas overlooking the Adriatic. I wouldn't mind going to a place like that, someday. . . .

Just now we are passing through a plain of farmland. The fields are plowed, with nothing much growing yet. In the distance are woods and mountains.

Mutti lights her fourth or fifth cigarette in a row from the butt of the one she just finished.

"Hannerl, it's getting hard to breathe in here!" Vati opens the window, beats at the smoke to clear it out, then lights a cigarette himself. He almost never smokes! He says, "We're getting near the border."

There's a mountain straight ahead. It looks as though we are heading right into it.

For a second everything went black. We'd gone into a tunnel. "That's Szentgotthard," Vati said. "The border runs through the middle."

Mutti put her hand on mine. Hers felt damp.

The compartment lights came on. Out the window there was blackness, and our reflections in the glass.

With no space around it the train was suddenly roaring

thunder-loud. I thought, What if this mountain collapses on top of us, and we never get out of here?

Never get out, never get out, thundered the wheels on the tracks.

But already there was light.

"Inge, put that book away now," my father said sharply, and fumbled with the catch of the briefcase where the documents are. "We'll be at Marburg in a moment."

Marburg was its name when this whole region still belonged to the Austro-Hungarian Empire. Now its name is Maribor.

First came the Austrian, I mean the Ostmark, border guards. They checked our exit permits and Mutti's pocketbook and Vati's wallet and looked through our hand luggage and satisfied themselves we weren't smuggling money out.

Then came the Yugoslav border guards, one thin and tall, one stocky. They looked at my parents' passports. (I'm included on my mother's.)

The stocky guard frowned and said, "Where are your visas?"

"We don't need any," said Vati in an aloof voice, but beads of sweat were on his forehead. "Here." He showed the baptismal certificates.

The guards talked rapidly together in Croatian or Slovenian.

"The regulations have been changed," said the stocky one. "Now everybody must have a visa."

"Just like that? What do you expect us to do?" Vati asked indignantly. He put his hand to his face so the guard wouldn't see the sweat running down.

"That is rather inconvenient," said my mother brightly. "I'm surprised! I saw the consul just the other day." Somehow she made it sound as though the consul were a close friend of ours. "Why didn't he tell me? We have these reservations, you see, here at this lovely resort." She took out the brochure about the hotel and showed it to the guards.

"Nevertheless, madame, visas are required."

"Well, what would you like us to do?" Mutti gave her ripply laugh. "Go all the way back to Vienna for visas? We'd miss three days of our stay! They'd give our rooms away! Here"—she looked up at the stocky guard from under her eyelashes— "would you like one of these? They're Egyptian tobacco."

The guard took a Memphis and had a short conference with his colleague, who, we thought, didn't speak German.

But he did. "Come with me a moment," he said to Vati. Vati put his coat on. They went out.

The stocky guard sat himself down next to my mother.

For the next five minutes, or however long, my heart pounded so loud that if he hadn't been chatting to her they could have heard it, I was sure.

Then Vati came back, without the tall, thin guard. He showed the stocky one the passports. Now they had visas stamped in.

The guard smiled. "May I take another cigarette for my colleague?"

Mutti held the pack out.

He helped himself to five. "Welcome to Yugoslavia, and pleasant vacation!" He left.

"That's a thriving little business they are doing," said Vati. "Those visas cost forty-five schillings."

"What a coincidence," Mutti said. Forty-five schillings is exactly how much money we had, among the three of us. The Nazis let every Jew leaving the country take fifteen schillings out, not more. Of course the Yugoslavs know that.

So now we don't have a groschen, or a dinar (that's Yugoslav money). But who cares? We're out, we're safely across! The Löwbergs are meeting us at the station in Zagreb, we'll be there in an hour. We'll stay with them, they want us to, till we can have a place of our own.

My parents were standing in the middle of the compartment, lurching when the train lurched, laughing, saying each other's names, and hugging each other. Then Vati said, "Come, Inge," and each held out one arm to me, and I got into their hug.

Afterword

Like Inge Dornenwald, I was a child in Nazi Austria. My best friend's name was Lieselotte. My mother broke her hip while skiing, my grandfather scrubbed sidewalks with a toothbrush, on his knees. And—thanks to luck, and to my parents' courage— we escaped the same way the Dornenwalds did and came to America.

Readers often ask me: "Is Inge really you?"

Yes and no. I was a lot like Inge. But Inge is older, thirteen. She goes to *Gymnasium*. She's smart, she understands what's going on much better than I did. I was nine, in third grade (and got kicked out for being Jewish!). Besides, Inge does not have a sister. But I do. My sister was thirteen back then, and smart, and in *Gymnasium. She* was a lot like Inge. . . .

Inge is the two of us in one.

Readers also ask me: "Are you still friends with Lieselotte?"

No. I really did have a best friend by that name; her father was a Nazi big shot; and they moved to Munich. Everything else about the Lieselotte in the book—her letters from Munich, her return to Vienna—I made up. It's fiction. What's true is her character. I based it on a classmate of my sister's, a gutsy girl who hated the Nazis. When war broke out, she joined the Austrian resistance. She lives in Vienna. My sister lives in New York. But they've stayed in touch these many years, and are still best friends.

Another question I've been asked, and one I've asked myself: "What made me write this book?"

I knew I needed to write it. Why did I keep putting it off? Wondering about that reminded me of friends I had in high school—close, good friends, all refugees like me. We talked endlessly about any subject, except one: where we'd come from, what happened there, and how we got out (in my case, nearly not!).

The deepest reason for our friendship was the background we shared. Yet talking about it was taboo. We were probably scared, even though our lives in Europe were behind us. I know *I* had fears locked up inside—fears all the scarier because they were vague, dating back to Vienna and things I'd only dimly understood.

Most of all, we wanted to be popular, do well, and have fun, like everybody else. We pushed aside what made us different, and told ourselves it didn't matter. We were Americans now.

So, for many years, I did not write this book.

Belatedly, after writing other books, and visiting Austria twice as a tourist, with my American husband and kids, I pulled my head out of the sand and faced the truth: what happened when the devil came to Vienna mattered very much to me.

I started by doing historical research. Then I interviewed my parents and everyone else I knew who had experienced that time in Austria. Finally, I was ready to write about what living under Nazism was like.

It all happened long ago, but it still matters. I hope it makes readers ask themselves: "If someone like Hitler came to power here and now, how would I feel? What would *I* think and do?"

—*Doris Orgel, New York City, 2004*

Note to the Reader

Roughly 180,000 Jews lived in Vienna in 1938. Some 100,000 fled. In 1945, after the war ended, only 5,000 of the remaining 80,000 had survived.